"You look adorable in bubbles. May I come in?" Cody asked.

Liza reached for a towel, trying to keep everything vital submerged. "You have a way of ruining a beautiful bubble bath. Why don't you lie down on the—damn, I can't reach it—couch, while I dress?"

He handed her the towel, making a great show of keeping his eyes averted. "I don't want to lie down. I've been flat on my back for two days."

"I'm not getting out of here until you leave," Liza said gently. "Do you want to be responsible for me catching pneumonia?"

Cody sighed. She looked so soft and warm and luscious with her knees drawn up to her chin and the bubbles floating in little islands around her.

A fever gave a man excuses to do the most outrageous things.

"I'll go," he promised, "very soon now."

He knelt beside the tub in one fluid motion, taking her chin in his hand and drawing her toward him with gentle force. His lips met hers, caressing, demandin~~~~~ merized by the exqui~~~~~

D1521555

Courtney Ryan

Courtney Ryan began writing at the age of six, when she was given her first typewriter. Although her typing hasn't improved much since then, she now enjoys "seeing my fantasies—minus spelling errors, bless my editor—come to life on the printed page." She gives credit to "a very handsome and understanding husband" who joins her in research for her romantic novels. Courtney lives with her husband and children in Utah.

Dear Reader:

Along with this month's beautiful weather, May also brings you two of the finest authors Second Chance at Love has to offer. I know you'll be captivated by the romantic sparring between two of Courtney Ryan's most electric characters. And Dana Daniels holds true to form—setting up her two unsuspecting characters for a chance meeting that will forever change their lives . . .

Love and magic abound in the beautiful Mexican locale of *Cody's Gypsy* (#438) by Courtney Ryan. Liza Carlisle has a bad case of wanderlust. When her worried father hires Detective Cody Davis to find Liza, Cody assumes she's an irrepressible dilettante. But when he finds her in Mexico, she turns out to be an adorable gypsy with a carefree spirit and a contagious sense of fun. It doesn't take long for Cody to fall under her spell. But will Liza slow down long enough to let Cody catch—and keep her? You'll fall in love, as Cody and Liza do, in this sensual and breezy romance!

Talk about fate. Shelly Hayes is just filling in for a friend at the local gas station when gorgeous millionaire Tyler Lightfoot's car pulls up. And talk about magnetic! Before she knows it, Shelly's in Tyler's arms—and then, somehow, she's everywhere else he goes after that! Of course, that's just fine with Tyler. But who are all these other guys in Shelly's life? Who's Stanley? And why does Tyler find himself reacting in ways he never dreamed of anytime Shelly is near, or not near? Don't miss Dana Daniels' *The Lady Eve* (#439) for the romantic climax to this delightful romance.

And this month, Berkley brings you some truly wonderful titles. At the top of the list is *Dance of the Gods* by Norma Beishir. From the ultra-exclusive reaches of Malibu and Beverly Hills, to the glittering playgrounds of New York and Paris, Meredith Courtney, an accomplished newscaster, and wealthy tycoon Alexander Kirakis, share a passion and fantasy come true. Enter Tom and Elizabeth Ryan,

Hollywood's legendary director and his beautiful wife, whose tragic and shocking past could destroy Meredith's newfound love . . . Stephanie Blake, the author of *Texas Lily,* has written a sweeping new saga of one woman's triumph of love and hope in *This World is Mine.* Holly Cavendish came to America from the streets of London and went on to gain local prominence as a journalist. But in her heart she longed for more, a deep and genuine love. And it seemed that Dick Cullen, her striking co-worker, could offer it—but dare she open up to so all-consuming a passion? And, finally, the latest novel from the *New York Times* bestselling author of *Interview With the Vampire* and *The Vampire Lestat*—*Belinda,* by Anne Rice writing as Anne Rampling. Renowned illustrator Jeremy Walker seems to have it made, but the trappings of success are wearing thin. He is searching for an escape until extraordinary magic enters his life . . . Belinda. She's the answer to his deepest desires. He is lured into a world of spirited passion and obsessive love. He *must* possess all the secrets locked in her past—and the startling truth behind a Hollywood legend.

Well, there you have it! A wonderful assortment of delectable reads to help you usher in the Spring. Here's wishing you a wonderful month until we meet again . . .

Happy reading!

Hillary Cige

Hillary Cige, Editor
SECOND CHANCE AT LOVE
The Berkley Publishing Group
200 Madison Avenue
New York, NY 10016

SECOND CHANCE AT LOVE™

COURTNEY RYAN
CODY'S GYPSY

BERKLEY BOOKS, NEW YORK

CODY'S GYPSY

Requests for permission to make copies of any part of the work
should be mailed to: Permissions, Second Chance at Love, The
Berkley Publishing Group, 200 Madison Avenue, New York, NY
10016.

First edition published May 1988

ISBN: 0-425-10743-4

"Second Chance at Love" and the butterfly emblem are trade-
marks belonging to Jove Publications, Inc. The name "BERK-
LEY" and the "B" logo are trademarks belonging to Berkley
Publishing Corporation.

Second Chance at Love books are published by
The Berkley Publishing Group
200 Madison Avenue, New York, NY 10016

Printed in the United States of America

10 9 8 7 6 5 4 3 2 1

With thanks to D.H.M.,
my enthusiastic, emotional,
encouraging advisor

Chapter

1

CODY DAVIS ARRIVED in Mazatlán, Mexico, at one o'clock P.M. on November 3. Cody was a fearless police detective, a black belt in karate, and a frequent contributor to the Red Cross blood drives, but he was a poor traveler. The three-hour flight from Denver was a grueling exercise in mind over stomach. Fearless police detectives did not disgrace themselves by succumbing to motion sickness—particularly when the stewardess assigned to first class was a stunning Kathleen Turner look-alike. Cody suffered heroically, lunching on Dramamine pills and ginger ale while the rest of the passengers enjoyed chicken parmesan. By the end of the flight, Cody's complexion was cream cheese, but he was on first-name terms with the stewardess, and dignity had been maintained. With some effort he managed to allow a mother and her young child to exit the plane ahead of him before bolting for solid ground.

Mazatlán's air terminal at the height of the tourist season was a furor of sound and color. A steady stream of sun-fried vacationers passed through the departure gates, two-legged packhorses laden with native blankets, woven baskets, and straw hats. New arrivals, marked by their winter-white skin and Nikon necklaces, pressed through the narrow corridors like salmon swimming upstream. Having survived the friendly skies, Cody's irrepressible spirits rose to the challenge of Mexican customs. Impulsively, he tried out his high-school Spanish on a customs official, only to be met with a turtle-eyed stare.

"You don't speak Spanish?" Cody asked.

"*Sí, señor,*" the man replied laconically. "It is *you* who do not speak Spanish. Business or pleasure?"

"Pleasure," Cody replied. *Immediately after I complete my business,* he amended silently.

The customs official tapped a pen against his teeth, studying Cody intently. Cody returned the look, bright-eyed and disarming. Privately, he acknowledged that his appearance might arouse some curiosity. At the moment, he had his left arm in a sling, a bandage on his forehead, and a pastel-colored jawbone. Nothing too serious—injuries sustained in the line of duty, little mementoes of bad timing. In search of a chocolate doughnut, he'd walked smack into the middle of a convenience-store robbery. The odds had been unfair but not impossible: one policeman against two snockered teenagers—easy to subdue—and a perfectly lucid, knife-wielding Rambo clone who was not. Cody took some satisfaction in the fact that Rambo was still in the hospital.

"It was a rough flight," Cody said.

The customs official stamped his papers with some force and waved him through.

Cody thoroughly enjoyed the ride along the coast from the airport to his hotel. Like the majority of cabs in Mazatlán, the white Plymouth was independently owned, a 1961 sedan minus windows and air-conditioning. Cody didn't mind the sweltering humidity in the least after the Siberian landscape he'd left behind in Colorado. The ocean was calm and sun-shot with diamonds, the palm trees swayed in unison, and the women all appeared to be uncommonly beautiful. A few hours of feeling green thirty thousand feet above the ground was a small price to pay for a vacation in paradise. From this point on, cares and worries would vanish with every wave that rolled across the sugar-white sand. This sun-drenched, smiling country was just waiting to nurse Detective Cody Davis back to health.

But first things first.

"I wonder if you could help me," Cody said to the cab driver. "I'm looking for someone, a young woman. She's working in a place called Juan's Cantina. Have you heard of it?"

"My English is bad, *señor*."

Cody dangled a ten-dollar bill over the seat. He hadn't yet had time to exchange his money for pesos, but the cab driver didn't seem to mind. His grasp of the English language improved dramatically.

"I remember now, *señor!* There is such a place— Señor Juan's Cantina, by the waterfront where the cruise ships dock. Big tourist place, crowded every night. Best chimichangas in Mazatlán. You wish to go there?"

"No... just take me to the hotel. I'll try Juan's chimichangas tonight." Cody leaned back in the seat, his mouth curving with little commas on each side.

This was going to be easier than he'd thought.

"The man is no good," Pilar whispered. "I tell you, I have intelligence about these things. That one is not to be adjusted."

"Trusted," Liza corrected, balancing a tray of margaritas with one hand and holding a basket of warm tortilla chips with the other. Pilar had an extensive English vocabulary, but she still needed a bit of work on the basics. "The man is not to be trusted."

"That is what I *said*." Pilar shrugged, propped both hands on her hips, and shook back her wild black curls. "If you would listen! He is a criminal, Liza, I can see it in his face. I've been watching him ever since he came in. He stares and stares at you. Also, I believe he has a gun in his pants."

"Oh, my." Liza's smile bloomed as she tried to locate Pilar's "criminal" in the dun-colored room. "Where is this desperado?"

"I told you, in the corner by the giraffe."

The restaurant's decor was eclectic, to say the least. Stuffed animals abounded, semi-obscene T-shirts graced the walls, and battle-scarred piñatas swung from the ceiling. Tourists thrived on the happy confusion and the superb Mexican cuisine, often standing shoulder to shoulder at the bar for the better part of an evening when a table wasn't available. Liza lifted her chin to get a better view of the corner table, meeting the unblinking stare of the six-foot giraffe over the sunburned throng. "I can't see a thing, Pilar. You're letting your imagination run away with you."

Pilar frowned, momentarily distracted. "How can that be? Imagination running?"

"Figure of speech, I'll explain later. I've got to serve these drinks before I drop them."

"I'll do it." Pilar quickly snatched the tortilla chips and the tray of drinks, sending a margarita tidal wave spilling over the frosted glasses. "You watch that man. Keep both your eyes on him. He is a villain. I feel trouble coming."

There was no use arguing. Liza was only too familiar with Pilar's passion for drama. The young woman had dreams of becoming a movie star, and every word she spoke, every expression that crossed her face, was calculated to touch the emotions of her audience. Last night Pilar had insisted that the gentleman at the bar wearing Bermuda shorts and the bright Izod shirt was actually Julio Iglesias. Tonight public enemy number one was sitting by the stuffed giraffe. Resigned and amused, Liza leaned against the wall near a potted palm and slipped her aching feet out of her shoes. Across the room the giraffe seemed to offer a sympathetic smile, and Liza winked at him conspiratorially. It was nice to be appreciated, considering the blisters simmering between her toes and the bruises blooming on her hips. Liza made a mental note: The next time one of Juan's waitresses called in sick, she wouldn't be quite so eager to offer her services. Normally, she sang in the bar on Friday and Saturday nights and helped Juan balance the receipts every Monday. She enjoyed the work, and earned enough money to finance her extended stay in Mazatlán. Still, none of that had prepared her for the jovial, bottom-pinching animal known as the Hungry Tourist.

A limbo contest between several bright-eyed customers at the bar was attracting a growing audience. The crowd between Liza and the stuffed giraffe quickly thinned out, providing her with an excellent view of Pilar's villain.

She drew a single breath out of rhythm with the others. She couldn't explain the profound sense of disorientation she felt. Watching him watch her, she had fleeting impressions of his coloring and build. His face was narrow, the contours clean and refined, the cheekbones high and sculptured, his wide mouth stretched in a wry twist that might or might not have been the beginning of a smile. The hair was thick and layered in choppy waves, the color of strong coffee. But it was his eyes that held her, eyes that transformed a merely attractive countenance into something extraordinary. Deep set and heavy lidded, they appeared soft and dark in the shadows, perhaps brown or deep, deep green. There were secrets in those eyes, and a strange curiosity, and something else. Almost subconsciously, Liza registered the flesh-colored bandage on his forehead and the white sling on his arm. Ah, yes, the injuries alone were enough to kick Pilar's Technicolor imagination into double time.

And still he watched her.

From her posture of frozen attention, she saw him raise his hand and gesture to her. Confusion, or perhaps a more intense emotion that she couldn't define, made her avert her eyes until she remembered that she was a waitress. Rather, she was *pretending* to be a waitress. If the man was trying to catch her eye, it was probably because he had been sitting at his table for over twenty minutes without having his order taken. True, he was seated at one of Pilar's assigned tables, but as long as the young Mexican woman imagined he concealed a weapon in his pants, his chances of being served were slim at best.

Enough already. Liza summoned a smile and hitched up the elasticized neckline of the peasant blouse she had borrowed from Pilar. Whimsically, she decided she must be in an unusually restless stage of her life. It wasn't like her to join Pilar on a flight of fancy. The customer at the corner table was a man of considerable presence, but hardly the type to incite a brawl or consort with criminals. More than likely he was a passenger from one of the cruise ships, who had taken a nasty tumble on the promenade deck. If there were any justice in the world, it was only fair that such a physically appealing man should also be a klutz.

She made her way to the table, fumbling in the pocket of her skirt for her pencil and order pad. No pencil. Where had she put it? "How are you this evening?" she asked, fishing in the other pocket.

"Fine, thank you," he said, his eyes continuing their serene observation. Liza observed that his eyes were a deep forest green, glittering with unknown thoughts. "Misplaced something?"

"My pencil." Liza felt more than a little self-conscious as she searched behind her ears through wispy tendrils of honey-gold hair. Earlier in the evening she had secured her leonine mane with a huge ivory comb, but now the silky strands were working loose, collapsing on her forehead and neck. "I can't imagine where I put it."

"Perhaps with your shoes?" he suggested, one raised eyebrow wrinkling the bandage on his forehead.

Ah, a comedian. Her bare toes twitched, but she didn't blink. Never, never again would she begrudge a waiter or waitress a generous tip. They earned every cent. "I was just taking a break and slipped them off," she explained, shrugging the traveling neckline of her blouse into place and hitching up her skirt. Wearing Pilar's clothes was something of a challenge. Liza wished she had a pair of suspenders to keep everything on target. "I'm afraid I left my pencil at the bar. If you'll just excuse me one moment...?"

"I'm not going anywhere," he said.

Something in his tone prickled through Liza as she turned away. *I'm not going anywhere.* She found herself glancing back over her shoulder, meeting his curious, searching gaze. She realized with a little jolt that he was studying her, watching, searching. And something told her he wasn't entirely happy with what he saw.

What have we here? Cody continued to stare after her, startled, fascinated, confused. Liza Carlisle wasn't what he had anticipated. He'd seen photographs of her before he'd left Denver of course, dozens of them. Her father had supplied him with a family album when Cody had agreed to Dr. Carlisle's little proposition. It seemed so simple at the time. Thanks to the chocolate doughnut fiasco, Cody faced six monotonous weeks of medical leave from the police force while he convalesced. Six weeks of staring at the walls of his apartment and playing slam-dunk in the wastebasket with beer cans. Six weeks of presoaking his shirts to try to remove the stains from his shoulder holster. Six weeks of excruciating boredom while the bad guys ran wild.

Dr. Carlisle had a better suggestion. After operating on Detective Davis twice in two years, he was well aware of his patient's low threshold of boredom. The good doctor prescribed two weeks on the sunswept beaches of Mexico—all expenses paid. And while in Mazatlán, the frustrated detective could put his skills to good use by going on a discreet fact-finding mission.

In law-enforcement lingo, Cody was going to be a snitch.

Suddenly, an ear-splitting crash was heard above the din in the restaurant. Instinctively, Cody tensed, scanning the crowd until he discovered the source of the commotion. A busboy sat dazed on the floor near the bar, surrounded by dozens of broken glasses. Liza Carlisle was hovering over him, patting his shoulder, apologizing, stooping to clean up the debris from what looked like a head-on collision. Her hair was wild, her blouse stopped just this side of indecent, and her eyes were lush with graphic emotion. Embarrassment. Amusement. Exasperation. Those wide, haunting eyes hid nothing. Cody couldn't remember the last time he had seen a woman who didn't bother with defenses.

Her appearance intrigued him—and baffled him. She hardly looked like the demure young miss featured in the Carlisle family photo album. Where was the posture-perfect Barbie doll drowning in ruffles at her senior prom? When Dr. Carlisle had confided that he hadn't heard from his daughter for over six weeks, Cody had drawn his own conclusions. The Carlisles were extremely wealthy, and Liza was their only child. It was obvious from the family album—which was actually a pictorial tribute to every breath little Liza took—that their daughter had been shamelessly indulged from kindergarten through college. It was hardly surprising to Cody that she had chosen to spend her life flitting from one corner of the world to another, visiting her parents only three or four times a year and writing infrequently. Princesses were not brought up to respect the golden rule.

Though normally Cody made it a practice to mind his own business, he found himself sympathizing with Dr. Carlisle's concerns. The last letter the family had received from their wandering gypsy had been mailed from Mazatlán a month before, and mentioned plans of performing at Juan's Cantina during the tourist season. As she didn't elaborate, Dr. Carlisle's imagination began working overtime. He couldn't help but wish for just a few more details on Juan, the cantina, and the performance. And who better to ferret out the information than Detective Davis?

Now, looking at Liza Carlisle, Cody drew a deep breath and leaned back in his chair. If it wasn't for that full, enigmatic mouth, so ripe with promise, and those startling golden-brown eyes that had looked at him from a hundred photographs, he would have sworn he was looking at the wrong woman. Spoiled? Hardly, with her face flushed with exertion and a smear of taco sauce staining her skirt. Her tawny-gold hair was romantic and wild, but Cody would bet his next paycheck she hadn't seen the inside of a beauty salon in a year. She wasn't a waitress—at least, not an experienced waitress. She wasn't "performing."

Cody was confused. He hated to be confused.

Liza helped the busboy to his feet, then hurried over to Cody with a spectacular, apologetic smile. It was one of the finest smiles Cody Davis had seen in a long time.

"I'm sorry," she said. "It's been one of those nights. Have you decided what you'd like?"

You. Cody's mind formed the word while he hastily scanned the menu for the first time. Though he looked at the list of entrées, he saw only the golden-brown eyes that somehow managed to combine rich sensuality with clear, compelling honesty. He knew himself fairly well, so this sudden tumult she caused in his body came as no surprise. Even splattered with taco sauce, she was a very attractive woman, not to mention something of a mystery. A lethal combination.

"Guacamole salad and a chicken chimichanga," he said.

"Excellent choice. Anything to drink?"

She had amazing skin, Cody thought, silky-smooth, luminous, beautifully sun-kissed. Dr. Car-

lisle's photographs did not do justice to that skin.
Three—no, four freckles dotted the tip of her nose.
Dr. Carlisle's photographs didn't do justice to that
nose, either.

"Yes," Cody said, wondering what the hell she had
asked him.

She waited, idly musing about the bandage on his
forehead and the bruises along his jaw. And waited.
Then: "*What* exactly would you like to drink? Coffee?
Beer? A soft drink?"

"A beer will be fine," Cody said, passing his hand
over his eyes. He felt a little . . . shaky. Like at his
graduation from junior high school, dammit, when
he had first seen Julie Sue Babbit overflowing her
strapless velveteen gown.

"A beer it is." Liza eyed him curiously, noticing
that the plum-colored shadows on his jaw were distinctly knuckle-shaped. Hmmmm. Not a cruise-ship
passenger after all. Fist fights were a no-no on the
love boats. What was it about an injured man that
was so appealing? Suddenly, she was humming with
the old Florence Nightingale instinct, itching to
smooth that too-long hair, tempted to exchange his
chimichanga for a nourishing bowl of chicken soup.
"Would you like chips and soup—chips and *salsa*—
while you wait?"

"That would be fine." Detective Davis decided it
was high time he started detecting. "You must be
American," he said casually.

Her reflective gaze lifted to his. "And you must be
accident prone."

"Actually, I'm extremely lucky." That was certainly
what her father kept telling him. "You don't know

how good it is to hear a western accent. Let me guess. California? Arizona?"

Liza was disappointed. So far this evening, no less than four well-oiled, glassy-eyed males had preceded a come-on with a guessing game as to her home state. Being the only American employee—and a blonde, at that—in Juan's Cantina had its disadvantages. She didn't know why, but she'd expected this particular man to be different. "Getting warmer," she said. "Colorado." *And next he'll tell me he has an aunt living in Colorado, or a brother.*

"No kidding." Cody whistled softly, green eyes tucking at the corners with a smile. "What a coincidence. I was born in Colorado. Little town called Golden. Have you heard of it?"

"'Fraid not. I'll just run and get your salad."

He watched her hurry away with the smile dropping off his face by degrees. So much for detecting. He must be having an off night.

Liza brought his salad, drink, and entrée in a whirlwind rush that left no time for conversation. Cody picked at his food, barely tasting the best chimichanga in Mazatlán. His gaze traveled with Liza around the room for the next sixty minutes, clicking off details. She misplaced her pencil two more times. She slipped off her shoes whenever she was waiting at the bar for an order, rocking back and forth on the balls of her feet. She disappeared into the ladies' room and emerged with her hair twisted in a tight knot on her head. Fifteen busy minutes later, the knot was just a memory, and her tangled curls danced in the smoky breeze from the ceiling fans.

Nice, very nice. He liked her better with her hair down.

"Liza," he said softly, because he wanted to hear how it sounded. Which was a strange thing to do, even for unpredictable Cody Davis. His smile came oh-so-slowly as he watched her blouse slide off her shoulder for the umpteenth time. The light reflecting from the candles on the tables made her skin look hot and golden. The warm curve of her breast was visible for a brief moment before she twitched the elasticized neckline back into place. Cody spared a fleeting regret for all the dark-eyed Mexican beauties he was destined never to know. It was not to be—at least, not this trip. Liza Carlisle's wandering blouse and winsome smile had suddenly changed his plans. Fortunately, Cody was adaptable. In his profession, it was essential to be adaptable.

He wasn't quite sure just when he became aware of the fact that he wasn't the only man in the room watching Liza. Oh, men were *noticing* her, the way men always notice a beautiful, vibrant woman. But there was something different about the Old Spice preppie at the bar. He was obviously American: tall, blond, and tanned to a rich Coppertone brown. He wore a complacent look of leonine confidence, and his shaggy mane of hair was burned white by the sun. Not your typical tourist—he was minus the sunburn and the Bermuda shorts. He wore pleated linen slacks and a white cotton shirt that managed to look breezy and incredibly expensive at the same time. He had been ignoring his margarita for over an hour. Elbows propped on the bar, chin resting on his knuckles, his lively blue eyes followed Liza with un-

abashed interest. Whenever she passed within ear-
shot, he made some comment that invariably
brought a smile and a reproachful shake of her head.

Cody might have learned to be adaptable, but he
didn't enjoy complications. The blond lounge lizard
was a complication.

Cody resisted the occasional attempts to clear his
table, hanging on to his cold chimichangas and his
flat beer until closing time—which happened to be
one in the morning in party-happy Mazatlán. Like-
wise, Liza's not-so-secret admirer at the bar exchanged one untouched drink for another and
continued to cheerfully eat her with his eyes. No
subtlety, Cody thought with mild disgust. No finesse.
And what the hell did he keep saying to her to make
her laugh like that?

Cody was still mulling over his options when Liza
presented him with his check and a complimentary
thimble-sized glass of Kahlúa and cream.

"I hope you enjoyed your dinner," she said du-
biously, glancing down at the chimichangas still nestled in a rubbery bed of cold cheese. "Juan's food is a
bit spicy for some people. It takes a little getting
used to."

"The food was fine." Cody's tone was abstracted.
The lights in the restaurant were being extinguished
one by one. He debated with himself about his next
step. Unlike the airline stewardess, Liza didn't seem
particularly sympathetic to his postoperative condition. Neither was she eager to discuss their mutual
home state. Which left only his charming personality
and cunning mind to win the lady over, gather a little
information for Dr. Carlisle, and deal with the com-

plication sitting at the bar. *Ergo,* he uncoiled the warmest smile he could muster with a sore jaw. "I suppose I've never really liked eating alone. I could starve to death before my vacation is over."

"I doubt that."

I doubt that? So much for charm. In a rare and bold move, Cody attempted the direct approach. "Is there any chance you'd take pity on a lonely tourist and come out for a drink with me?"

It wasn't Liza's first invitation of the evening. The rotund aluminum-siding salesman from Boise had offered dinner and a "whale of a good time." The purser from the *Angela Lauro* had suggested a personalized tour of the officers' cabins. One glassy-eyed tourist had gone down on his knees and proposed marriage. An interesting variety of propositions, not one of which was remotely tempting. Until now.

This man was . . . rather appealing in a cocky, boyish sort of way. Her gaze made an involuntary traverse of his body, touching with fierce brevity on the long, muscular thighs giving exquisite shape to the biscuit-colored jeans. Not so boyish, after all. "I don't think so," she said, surprised that the words were so hard to come by. "Never accept rides, candy —or drinks—from strangers. A lesson learned at my mother's knee."

For a moment, Cody visualized prim Mrs. Carlisle, with her pearl chokers and tailored linen suits. Yes, indeed, he could see her instilling in Liza all kinds of fine lessons. His wayward mouth held the trace of a wry smile. "Do you do everything your mother told you to do?"

"As far as my mother knows." She assumed a

wide-eyed gravity that was adorable. Suddenly, Cody
wanted to touch her in the worst way, to smooth her
sun-streaked hair or touch his finger to her cheek.
Just to *touch* her...

"I'm hardly a stranger," he said. He had no idea
how she accomplished it, if the effect was calculated,
but there was a sudden heat in his chest, as if everything inside had melted down into warm syrup.
"After all, we're both from Colorado. We're practi-
cally neighbors. What harm could there be in a simple drink?"

"My mother went into that in great detail," Liza
said. Her mouth lifted at the corners with a smile,
beguiling him. "And please don't tell me you're
harmless. I've never seen anyone with such an im-
pressive collection of battle scars. You're absolutely
terrifying."

"Now wait a minute." Cody was mildly indignant.
"My name is Cody Davis, and not only am I a God-
fearing citizen, but I also happen to be—"

"I really can't talk now." It amazed Liza that she
was actually considering strolling off into the balmy
Mexican night with a perfect—if rather bruised—
stranger. Through no fault of her parents', she was a
far cry from the reserved and fragile young women
the Carlisle family proudly produced generation after
generation. It had taken a bit of time and more than a
few mistakes, but Liza had finally come to terms with
herself. She would never be happy in a somber
Tudor mansion nestled snug on the edge of the Hidden Valley Country Club. She thrived on the unknown, and generally took her chances in the world
without a backward glance, but Mexico was Mexico,

and a bit of caution was only wise. "The cantina is closing in a few minutes and I still have several tables to clear. I have to keep moving before my legs give out on me."

"How can you say no to this poor bruised face?"

Liza started to smile, then caught herself. "I have a cold heart. Not to mention blisters on my feet."

"You're not making this easy," Cody said.

"Another lesson—"

"—learned at Mommy's knee. I know."

She hesitated briefly, her liquid brown eyes capturing him, effortlessly holding him. No woman should have a look that good, Cody thought, feeling himself getting lost in it. It wasn't fair.

"Well," Liza said.

"Well," Cody echoed, still hoping.

"The cashier will take your money up front. Enjoy your stay in Mazatlán." Liza spun on her heel, feeling an odd flush heating her skin. Twenty-six years old and still capable of becoming flustered. Just think of all the interesting things she had learned today. One, never wear heels when you wait on tables. Two, always stick your pencil in your bun, lest it be lost. Three, beware of charming tourists with sparkling green eyes and minor cuts and abrasions. They flustered.

Twenty minutes later, Liza walked barefoot into the warm night, shoes tucked firmly into her purse. Shaggy palm trees hung in the star-filled sky, nodding like reeds in the ocean breeze. Even at this hour of the morning, Avenida Olas Atlas was crowded with tiny, open-air taxis ferrying tired tourists to their hotels. Locals strolled in chattering family groups along the wide cobblestone walk that edged the busy boulevard, occasionally wandering down the sand embankment to play at the water's edge. The Mexican timetable never failed to amaze Liza. Here these children were laughing and playing at the wee hours of the morning, as if it were a Sunday afternoon in the park. Until the age of twelve, little Liza Carlisle had observed a strict nine o'clock bedtime.

Liza and her aching feet rested for a moment on a wrought-iron bench in the miniature garden outside of the cantina. After the furious pace in the restaurant, she felt oddly let down, almost irritable. It was as if the endless, intrinsic noise of life had suddenly dropped to a whisper. She didn't feel lonely, precisely . . . just *alone*. There were occasions when sultry tropical nights had their drawbacks. Suddenly, the warm bubble bath Liza had been eagerly anticipating lost a bit of its appeal.

A bright, euphoric voice broke through her thoughts. "See, how she leans her cheek upon her hand! Oh, that I were a glove upon that hand . . . oh, that I could remember the next line."

Liza recognized the lines from *Romeo and Juliet* and, curious, turned, locating the spouting poet on the low cinderblock wall that surrounded the restaurant. She let out the breath she had been holding, unaccountably disappointed. So. Cody Davis had quietly walked away, while the blond-on-bronze playboy from the bar was persevering. Funny. Of the two, she would have guessed Cody with the rainbow-colored jaw to be the more tenacious.

"It's you," Liza sighed, unable for a moment to remember his name. Something strange... "Willard?"

"*Mill-er,*" he said distinctly. He jumped down from the wall, brushing off the seat of his slacks. "Miller O'Keefe, as if I hadn't told you a hundred times already tonight. What do I have to do to make an impression on you?"

"Remember when you suggested a sunrise breakfast on the nude beach?" Liza asked sweetly.

He grinned, blue eyes dancing in the moonlight. "Ho-ho. That made an impression, did it?"

"You'll never know." Liza stood tiredly, scanning the street for an empty *pulmonia,* the local open-air taxis. The locals scorned the festive golf-cart taxis that dominated the boulevard, but tonight she simply couldn't face the twenty-minute walk home. She'd never been so tired in her life. "Thanks for the oratory, Romeo."

"I wasn't through," Miller said. "Well, I was through with *Romeo and Juliet.* I don't know it all that well. It's never been one of my favorites, too depressing. Would you like to hear something from *Twelfth Night?*"

"No." Where were those pushy taxi drivers when you needed them?

"I don't blame you. Not on an empty stomach. Where would you like to go for breakfast?"

Liza took two steps toward him, positioning her face six inches from his nose. "Read my lips, Miller. No breakfast. No nude beaches. No Shakespeare."

"You have beautiful lips," Miller offered sincerely. "How about pancakes? Not those tortilla things everyone keeps feeding me. Real, honest-to-goodness buttermilk fluffies with maple syrup. No one makes them the way I do."

"Of course they don't," Liza sighed. "And next you'll offer to take me back to your place—"

"My boat, actually. It's anchored in the harbor."

"—your boat, and whip up buttermilk fluffies." Liza pulled her shoes from her shoulder bag and slipped them on her feet. Tired or not, it was clearly time to start walking. Miller O'Keefe was likable in an odd sort of way, but she wasn't entirely certain he was operating on all eight cylinders. "Thank you for the offer, but I already have a date for breakfast." With Jean Naté bubbling bath oil.

"It's a real beaut," Miller said, falling into pace with her on the sidewalk. "You'll never forgive yourself if you miss this opportunity to—"

"Pumpkin! There you are."

Liza blinked. One minute the sidewalk was clear in front of them, the next minute Cody Davis was enfolding her in a one-armed, bone-crushing hug. She couldn't breathe. She was so astonished that she found it impossible to frame the words to put a halt to this confusing show of affection.

"I was afraid I'd missed you," Cody said, drawing back to ruffle her hair affectionately. He loved the look on her beautiful face—Bambi in Trauma. Possibly she hadn't yet realized that he was gallantly coming to her rescue. "You know I don't want you walking home alone, sugar doll. How many times have I told you to wait for me after work?"

Liza looked from Cody to Miller. "I don't—"

"I know you don't like to bother me." Cody turned to Miller with an exaggerated locker-room wink. "But hell's bells, what else are husbands for?"

Chapter

2

MILLER'S CAVERNOUS GRIN was drooping to one side. "Husband," he said. "How bitter a thing it is to look into happiness through another man's eyes."

"New friend, honey?" Cody asked Liza.

Liza nodded. Cody's good arm was draped around her shoulders, his fingers dangling over her left breast. Liza reached up with a loving hand and squeezed those dangling fingers until she heard his knuckles crack. "Cody, I'd like you to meet Miller O'Keefe."

"Ow," Cody murmured, carefully withdrawing his arm. For such a delicate little thing, the lady had a ferocious grip. "Are you vacationing in Mazatlán, O'Keefe?"

"I'm trying," Miller said on a sigh.

"When you were late picking me up tonight, *sweetheart*, Miller was kind enough to offer me"—

Liza paused for a satisfying moment, watching Miller wince—"rather, to see me home."

Cody knew damn well what Miller had offered Liza Carlisle, right down to a sunrise breakfast in the buff. Police work had taught him the inestimable value of eavesdropping. "Well, isn't that nice," he said. "I'm sorry I was late, honey. It's been one of those days."

Miller noted Cody's injuries with a wary eye. "Must have been one hell of a day."

"Mexico can be dangerous," Cody murmured. "There are all kinds of doors you can run into. *Comprende?*"

Miller received the message with an arched brow and a wry smile. "Only too well. My dear Mrs. Davis"—he paused, a little frown etching his nut-brown forehead—"I don't believe you ever told me your first name . . . ?"

"Liza," she said, deciding that he was handling the whole incident with charming aplomb.

Miller nodded, shoving his hands deep into the pockets of his slacks. "Liza. Something tells me I'll remember that name for a long time, rather like the Alamo. Liza, meeting you has been a frustrating but delightful experience. Davis, you're a fortunate man. Good night, all." Whistling, bright hair lifting and swirling in the breeze, he strolled away.

Cody had to grin when he recognized the tune: "The Impossible Dream."

"Liza what?" Cody asked when Miller's brave little melody faded. "I don't believe I caught your last name, pumpkin."

"I don't believe I threw it, sugar doll."

"Tacky, tacky. I expected better from you. In case you didn't notice, I just did you a favor. If I hadn't shown up, lord only knows what would have happened with that lunatic poet."

"I'll fill you in, then. Miller would have departed with a bruised ego—and possibly a bruised shin—and I would have returned to my humble abode. I'm a big girl, you know. I can take care of myself." Slanting Cody a sideways glance, she added carefully, "Bear in mind that you're the one wearing a sling. I'm not sure I can keep a straight face if you start lecturing me on self-defense."

"Give me a break," Cody said, digging into his jeans for his wallet. Before he could flip out his badge and thrill her with the story of the chocolate doughnut caper, a brightly fringed cousin to a golf cart squealed to a halt beside them.

"Taxi, *señora?*" the bored driver intoned. Obviously, it had been a long day, and he was wearying of being polite to tourists.

"*Sí! Gracias* from the bottom of my heart and the soles of my feet." Liza scrambled into the back seat of the cart, blinking in surprise when Cody joined her. "Just what do you think you're doing?"

Cody smiled sweetly, enjoying the cramped quarters. "Saving my reputation."

"Where to?" the driver asked.

It was odd, but Liza's bone-weary exhaustion seemed to have vanished in the breeze along with Miller's whistling. Suddenly, she had all the energy in the world, and didn't mind expending it in the least. She put both hands on Cody's thigh and shoved. He didn't budge.

"What do you think *you're* doing?" Cody asked.

"Removing you."

"You don't want to remove me," he said reproachfully. "You're enjoying yourself. You don't *want* to enjoy yourself—you'd much rather be angry—but you are."

Liza looked straight at him. Something in his compelling green eyes suddenly made her protests seem hollow. He was right. She wanted to be angry. Her golf cart had been commandeered by a stranger who called her pumpkin. Miller O'Keefe had wandered into the night believing she was married to a man who ran into doors. Had she had any desire whatsoever to participate in a sunrise breakfast in the buff, Cody would have made it impossible. She hadn't, but that was beside the point.

Logic told her that anger was the next step.

"So much for logic," she murmured blankly, her hands stilling on his leg. The night air was soft against her face, a canopy of palms rustled above them, and Cody's teasing, whimsical gaze was settling gently on her mouth. Her conscience whispered ever so faintly, sounding remarkably like her mother, but she let the dry scratching of the palms muffle the warning. Even now the utter pleasure of being in his company was a force to be reckoned with.

The lady was full of surprises, Cody thought. Most women would have wasted a great deal of precious time going through the paces of the outraged maiden. Liza simply looked at him with those otherworldly eyes and a curious sort of wonder. Cody couldn't take his eyes from the childish curve of her parted lips. He felt something whisper to life within him, a warm, gentle emotion that was totally unfamiliar. No, that wasn't entirely true. He'd experienced something similar just before he'd left for Mexico, when he'd visited a good friend who had recently had a baby. He'd held Jenny's terrifyingly small daughter in his good arm, tucking the little pink blanket around her with awkward hands, helping Jenny stick a tiny bow on her bald head with Karo Syrup. It occurred to him that he had been experiencing tenderness then, an emotion that had long been dormant in his life. Tonight he vaguely recognized a far more powerful strain of that same feeling, though he wasn't entirely sure of his capacity to deal with it. A mere thirty minutes with Jenny's baby had left his head swimming.

"I have something to show you," he said. "Something to put your mind at ease. Tell the driver where you want to go."

"I want to go home," Liza said, "and I've never had more trouble in my *life* getting there." She pulled her hands from his thigh and folded them prayerlike in her lap. Her palms tingled.

"I'll escort you."

Liza squirmed in her seat as the driver looked over his shoulder, fixing her with red-rimmed eyes. "It is late, *señorita*. It is also dangerous to park too long on Avenida Olas Atlas. You wish to go home or no?"

"Home or no?" Cody echoed innocently. Then, because he had no desire to end his life in a golf cart pile-up on Avenida Olas Atlas, he opened his wallet and dangled his badge in front of her nose. "I told you I was harmless. Now, do you trust me enough to escort you home, *señorita?*"

"You're a *policeman?*" Liza broke into a startled grin, and as her smile grew, so did his. She looked pointedly at the sling on his arm. "Are you a good policeman?"

"I'm a detective," Cody replied, lifting his hand to brush back a stray curl from her cheek. "And contrary to appearances, I'm a wonderful detective. Give the nice man your address, Liza, and I'll see you to your front door. You couldn't be in better hands."

His palm cradled the curve of her jaw, thumb brushing the delicate cleft in her chin while his sparkling gaze examined her face. Liza's throat was suddenly tight, and she felt a wave of heat rise in her chest. She was torn for a brief moment. She wanted to see this little adventure through, yet she wanted to put a lid on the past twelve frantic hours and shift her life back into mellow cruise. His smile sent a ripple of sweetness through her, but gave her no reassurance. She couldn't remember the last time a man had left her shaken with a touch of his hand. Not since Jeremy, and that was a lifetime ago. They had found each other during those urgent, hungry years at NYU, the naive debutante and the brooding would-be playwright. Liza had been on the run from the smothering demands made on an only child... frustrated, desperate for excitement, eager to try everything.

With Jeremy, her eyes had been opened.

He'd initiated her into the art of lovemaking, teaching her to believe in the rare qualities only Liza

Carlisle possessed. His friends in the theater had adopted her, exposing her to a bold sense of style and an unconventional outlook. And then Liza's precious freedom turned on her with a vengeance. Jeremy had worshiped her body and the shiny new soul he thought he had created. *Owned.* And his possessiveness had nearly destroyed her.

It was an ironic, expensive lesson in life for the wide-eyed young woman desperate for independence. It was not a lesson Liza was eager to repeat.

On the other hand, Cody Davis intrigued her. He made her smile. He surprised her. Liza was addicted to surprises.

"Only to the front door," she said. There were surprises, and then there were surprises.

He nodded solemnly. "Only to the front door."

She looked at him with angelic concentration, her lush golden eyes unconsciously tantalizing him. *Only to the door,* he told himself firmly. *Only to the door, only to the door . . .*

"Carlisle," she said softly.

"What?"

"My last name—Carlisle. My father's a surgeon, my mother's president of the Junior League, and I have a thing for bubble baths. Now I don't need to feel guilty. Technically, we're no longer strangers. We're . . . nodding acquaintances."

You might not feel guilty, but I'm having a hell of a problem. Cody retained his smile with some effort, uncomfortably aware of just how much he knew about his "nodding acquaintance." Her middle name was Marie. She'd had a bulldog named Figaro when she was growing up. She'd received a pony for her eighth birthday and a Porsche for her eighteenth. It was amazing how much information a family photo album could yield.

"Cody Patrick Davis," he said, trying to even the scales and shorten the guilt trip. "I'm thirty-four years old. I'm allergic to aspirin, I love to snow ski, and I have a thing for Vanna White. I'm basically reckless but still alive, which means either I'm a terrific police officer or just plain lucky. Enough?"

Liza smiled, settling happily into frivolity. "Enough. Do I have to call you Detective Davis?"

"No." Now he let his smile slip away without a struggle. He extended his hand slowly, touching the tip of her nose. "Just . . . call me Cody."

The driver slapped the steering wheel. "*Señor? Señorita!* The address, I beg of you. I wish to see my children again before they are grown."

"You heard the man," Cody said. "The address, *señorita.*"

Liza's "humble abode" was a small beach cottage snuggled between the Pacific Ocean and the Golden Palms condominium complex. The condominiums were a step or two down from the four-star tourist hotels a mile farther along the coast. They consisted of less than a dozen units arranged in a semicircle around a shadowy courtyard. A neon sign promised tranquillity, queen-size beds, and senior citizens' discounts. In the rear of the complex, wooden steps zigzagged to the beach through a leafy iguana heaven, festively illuminated by ropy strands of green Christmas-tree lights. Liza followed the steps to a small landing halfway through the zigs and zags, then took a sharp right and disappeared into a lush thicket alive with rustling noises.

True to his word, Cody was intent on seeing Liza to her front door. He didn't really mind the iguana traffic on the stairs. He hadn't realized they grew them quite so large down here, but they proved fast enough to whip across the weatherbeaten steps and into the surrounding greenery without interrupting his stride.

The green shadows that had swallowed Liza were another matter. Even with the help of the blinking Christmas-tree lights, Cody couldn't discover the faintest hint of a trail. Iguanas skittered, pebbles rattled, leafy boughs dipped into his hair. This was serious foliage.

"I give," he said, poking halfheartedly at a pizza-sized palm leaf. "If you're trying to ditch me, it would have been kinder to do it before I climbed down all those stairs."

"What?" Her voice was muffled by the rhythmic murmur of the ocean and the heavy green curtain between them.

"I can't find you." Cody slapped at a mosquito extracting a chunk of his neck. "You should have left a trail of bread crumbs or something."

"Go to your left. You'll see the path."

He went left, his Reeboks sending invisible creatures scampering. A couple of slaps in the face with a whippy green vine and the darkness opened up into a star-filled clearing with a small adobe building smack in the middle. Snow White's cottage, Mexican style, with a clay-tile roof and wrought-iron gratings over the windows. Liza waited on the front step beneath a stained-glass porch light that cast a rainbow over her pale hair.

"Civilization," Cody said, following the narrow cobblestone path that was blessedly iguana-free. "I was beginning to think I'd lost you."

"At night, this place looks like something from the Tarzan movies," Liza said. "During the day, it's pretty tame. You can see the ocean through the trees, hear the telephones ringing in the condominiums, watch the locals selling straw hats and blankets down on the beach. I like it better at night."

"Perfectly understandable," Cody murmured, pausing under the porch light to check the soles of his tennis shoes for squashed iguana. "Kind of reminds me of Denver at night. All those blind alleys and dark buildings. I'm never real sure what I'm walking into there, either." He looked up at Liza and smiled. "I like Denver better during the day."

Liza suddenly stepped closer. She seemed transfixed by something on his face.

"What is it?" Cody asked grimly, wondering if Liza kept tarantulas in her garden.

"You're bleeding!" she exclaimed, cupping his chin and turning his face to one side. "What on earth happened?"

Cody touched his cheek with his hand. His fingers came away sticky and wet. "I'm not sure. I think I was whipped with a vine trekking through your jungle. It's no big deal."

"It is in this climate. If you don't take care of open wounds immediately, infection can set in." Liza looked from the front door to Cody, chewing thoughtfully on her lower lip. Her eyes were wide and soft in the dim light, intuitive and compelling. It seemed like a long time before she said, "You'd better come in, then. I'll find something to put on it."

The latent tenderness that had been nagging at Cody all evening breathed new fire at her words. It was completely unexpected and far beyond the call of duty, this overwhelming desire to look after her. It was like meeting a stranger inside him, one he wasn't at all comfortable with.

"That's probably not the best idea you've had all night," he heard himself say tightly. "Did your mother skip the chapter on inviting strangers into your home?"

"We're not strangers." She hoisted her bag onto her shoulder and swung the front door wide. "We're nodding acquaintances, remember? You're the one who told me you were harmless—a law-abiding, God-fearing citizen. Besides"—this with a luscious smile thrown over her shoulder—"I'm not inviting you to dinner. I'm just disinfecting you."

"You don't lock your door?"

"Here? No. Why should I? There's no one to bother me." Crooking her finger at him, beckoning with whimsical brown eyes, she walked into the gray shadows of the house.

Cody took a moment to collect his thoughts. How wonderful it would be if he could attribute this bewildering new sensitivity to jet lag. A good night's sleep and he would wake refreshed and invigorated and cheerfully imperturbable. A lovable kind of guy with a basically self-centered lifestyle.

Watching the lights spear the gloom in the cottage, he knew it wasn't going to be so easy.

Inside, Liza was rummaging in what Cody assumed was the kitchen. He heard cupboards slam, water gurgling in the sink. While he waited, he looked curiously around the room, noting the plain furnishings. There was a steamer trunk doubling as a coffee table in the center of the living room, a beige velour sofa, a couple of skinny brass floor lamps, and a white wicker chair with a blue paisley cushion. There were no flower pots decorating the windowsill, no magazines arranged on the makeshift coffee table, no throw rugs to brighten up the cold tile floor. And books—Cody glanced at the empty wooden shelves in the corner, wondering where she put her books. Everyone kept some sort of reading material around the house. Even Cody, who had never been particularly fond of quiet evenings with a good book, kept a semirespectable collection of paperback novels.

"I found my first-aid kit," Liza announced, breezing into the room with an armful of medical supplies. "Well, I found *someone's* first-aid kit. It was under the sink behind the S.O.S. pads. Must have been left by the previous tenant."

"Have you lived here long?" Cody asked, wondering if she hadn't yet had time to add the personal touches most women seemed to enjoy.

"Quite a while. I moved in last August." Liza set out her equipment with the total concentration of a doctor preparing for an operation. Scissors. Gauze. Band-Aids. Iodine. Surgical tape. Hydrogen peroxide. "Come and sit down, and we'll take care of that scratch."

Cody was wary. "Don't you think you might be overdoing it?"

"I'm not going to *use* everything. I just grabbed everything in the kit. Now sit down and let Nurse Carlisle take a look at you."

Cody submitted to her ministrations, surrounded by the fragrance of her perfume and the sweet, narcotic sound of her breathing. Her thigh was a slight, erotic pressure against his, and the silky drift of her hair tickled his arm. If it hadn't been for the hydrogen peroxide she dabbed on his cheek, he could have stayed that way for hours.

"*Liza.*"

"Stings, doesn't it?" She caught her lush lower lip between her teeth, trying not to smile. "Can't be helped, Detective. We had to sterilize the wound."

"It's a scratch, Liza. Not a wound. Put that gauze down. You're not wrapping me up like a mummy."

"How about just a little butterfly bandage?"

"No." Cody had learned to be very firm in the hospital when the nurses had approached him with thermometers and specimen cups.

Liza settled back in the sofa with a sigh, studying him through gold-tipped lashes. "I wanted to be a nurse when I was six," she explained wistfully. "I *loved* Band-Aids. I used to go through dozens of them every week, caring for every imaginary cut and scratch in the neighborhood."

"Instead you found your calling in waitressing," Cody said, deadpan.

Amusement quirked the corners of her mouth. "I was terrible, wasn't I? Fortunately, I was just filling in for one of the waitresses who called in sick. I won't inflict myself on Juan's customers like that again. I could put him out of business."

"Then you don't work at the cantina regularly?" Cody was finding it difficult to concentrate on the conversation, Liza looking the way she did, the room filled with the sweet scent of her.

"Usually, I sing in the bar on weekends. I do a few numbers in Spanish, and the tourists don't seem to mind that I'm not a native. In fact, they like it. They're always requesting songs like 'New York, New York' or 'I Left My Heart in San Francisco.'"

Which explained the "performance." Strange that Liza's parents didn't clue him in on her singing ability. "So the bandage-happy nurse finally decided she wanted to be a singer?"

"No, no." Liza shook back her hair, tucking her bare feet beneath her on the sofa. "It was never that simple. Every time I turned around, I discovered a new interest. I wanted to be a nurse until I read *Black Beauty*. Then I wanted to be a jockey . . . then a stewardess. Almost every girl wants to be a stewardess at one time or another. I also went through a humanitarian stage when I wanted to join the Peace Corps . . . and so on and so forth."

"And now?"

She shrugged. "I suppose I'm taking each day as it comes. I have a college degree in fine arts, for what it's worth. I enjoy singing, but my voice is never going to set the world on fire. I've dabbled in oil painting. A year ago I worked as a research assistant for a historical romance novelist. I enjoyed that. We traveled all over Europe with four Yorkshire terriers."

A gleam of humor lit Cody's eyes. "Then you're not exactly a homebody."

"I'm afraid I'm a throwback to my ancestors. My mother's great-grandmother was a Basque gypsy. She sold healing herbs and told fortunes and followed carnivals and country fairs all over France and Spain."

"I find it extremely hard to believe that your mother—" Cody stopped abruptly, realizing he could hardly make a comparison between pink-cheeked Mrs. Carlisle with the puffy shoulder pads and a wandering Basque gypsy. As far as Liza knew, he had never met her mother. "It's hard to believe," he amended carefully, "that a woman who goes into great detail about the dangers of an after-dinner drink could be related to a gypsy fortune-teller."

"I know. Mother has a little difficulty with that, too." Liza felt wonderfully, beautifully relaxed, every muscle in her body stretching and saying *ahhh*. She watched Cody Davis beneath weighted lids, letting her senses absorb him. Emotion played with fascinating gentleness along the curves of his smile. The fuzzy white light from the lamps picked out the delicate bronze shading in his hair and the colorful bruises along his jaw. Even wrapped in a sling, the movements of his lean body were easy and unselfconscious. Suddenly, the force of his physical appeal hit her like a plank across the chest, stealing her smile and heating the skin stretched along her cheekbones. There didn't seem to be enough air in the room for the two of them.

Watching her, Cody sensed the withdrawal when it came. One moment she was frank and open, twirling a lock of hair around her finger while she confided her thoughts. The next moment she was sitting bolt upright, bare feet planted firmly on the ground, shoulders tense. She might as well have worn a stamp on her forehead: *anxiety attack*.

"Let me guess," Cody murmured. "It just hit you that you're sitting alone in your living room with a perfect stranger—excuse me, a *nodding acquaintance*—and you're afraid I'm going to pounce. *Sí, señorita?*"

His eyes in the soft light were bright, quizzical, offering to understand. Never before in her life had Liza seen eyes that could speak as eloquently as Cody's. "Something like that," she said, still feeling breathless, still struggling with hazy, tingling sensations. Then, with a flash of gentle humor, she added, "I suppose it never occurred to you that I might pounce on you?"

Startled, Cody managed a husky, "I can't say it did. Well, mind the arm and I'm game."

"Don't look at me like that. I'm not *going* to—I wouldn't dream of it. I was only teasing." Her sigh said, *I don't know what on earth's gotten into me tonight*. "It just kind of surprised me that I would even think such a thing. Normally, you're not the type of—never mind. I have a terrible habit of saying whatever comes into my mind, especially when I'm tired."

"Finish," Cody ordered grimly. A saccharine-sweet curve shaped his mouth as he added with exaggerated courtesy. "Please."

Her rueful smile hovered, wary and poignantly appealing. "I simply meant that I'm usually not attracted to . . . conservative types."

"*What?*"

Definitely the wrong thing to say, Liza thought, watching his nostrils flare. "It's just a first impression, mind you. I mean, you're a detective, so obviously you've had the same job for a number of years. You were born in Colorado, and now you're working in Denver, so I assume you've lived in the same state most of your life. And you wear a Timex."

"What the hell does my watch have to do with anything?"

"My father wears a Timex," Liza explained simply.

Here, then, was a brand-new experience for Detective Davis. No one had ever accused him of being conservative. Ever. The jeans in his closet outnumbered his slacks four to one. He drove a classic 1965 Mustang convertible that could go from zero to sixty in six seconds flat. He had two leather jackets, three little black books, and a first-place trophy from the Rocky Mountain Karate Classic. Not even to mention the fact that he spent his days and nights fighting for Truth, Justice, and the American Way.

No one called him conservative.

"I don't believe this," he muttered, raking his fingers through his hair. "I'm sitting here with a knife wound in my shoulder, and you're telling me I'm conservative."

Liza's face drained, her smile lost. "Knife?"

He'd said the words without thinking, more to himself than to her. Liza's stunned reaction caught him by surprise. Obviously, whatever she'd imagined as the cause of his injuries was a sight friendlier than a six-inch switchblade. "Actually, it was just a scratch," he said confidingly, wanting to erase the distress from her eyes. "I wear the sling strictly for appearances. I thrive on sympathy."

"You lie beautifully," Liza observed, her gaze still riveted on his shoulder. "So tell me. How did it happen?"

Cody sighed. "I was innocent. All I wanted was a chocolate doughnut. I walked into a Seven-Eleven store just as the bad guys yelled, 'Stick 'em up!' Poor timing all around."

"Bad *guys?* There was more than one?"

"Three. But two didn't count. They were too young to shave."

He smiled. Liza tilted her head to one side, curiosity about him stirring and growing within her. She knew instinctively that he was far more complex than he appeared, layer upon layer of substance and shadows. She could only imagine what it must cost him to keep his private struggles tucked away behind his teasing façade. She was a stranger to the sort of work he did, but she knew it would leave a man vulnerable in more ways than one. Disillusionment was inevitable in an amoral world, yet he gave no outward sign of it.

"I apologize for calling you conservative," she said, filling a silence that had stretched into awkwardness. "One look at your shoes and I should have known you were an individualist."

Cody glanced down at his battered, semi-white Reeboks with the fluorescent yellow laces. "True. Inspiring, aren't they? The laces glow in the dark. I think they scared the iguanas."

Another silence. Liza moved restively on the sofa. The atmosphere was unsteady, rippling with half-formed emotions. Cody realized they had exhausted their camaraderie for the time being, and a true gentleman would politely make his excuses and leave.

"Why don't you have any plants?" he asked.

Her brown eyes stretched wide. "What?"

"Plants. Green things with leaves. Most women have them hanging from the ceiling in those macramé things, or tucked into the windowsill with little bows around the clay pots."

"*Most* women? Really? Did you do a survey?"

Cody smiled, his eyes shimmering with introspective humor. "Perhaps I should rephrase that. Most *single* women." She continued to stare at him, prompting him to add, "A few single women."

"Well, I'm not a few *single* women," Liza said, looking defensively at her empty windowsill. "Besides, I don't like plants. They're too much work. And they always die when you try to move them."

"Hmmm. That explains the books."

"What books?"

"Your books," Cody said, lifting one long strand of golden hair that curled over the back of the sofa. "The ones you don't have on the coffee table or in the bookshelves. I'll bet you have them all packed away, ready to move on a second's notice."

Liza smiled sweetly, tapping the steamer trunk with one bare foot. "Books."

"What about figurines, knick-knacks, dried-flower arrangements, nifty little pillows you crocheted in Girl Scouts—"

"A true gypsy travels light." The air was still thick with feelings, warm and rich and strange, waiting to tease her whenever they ran out of words to fill the silence. "I suppose you're a regular homebody? Baseball trophies on your mantel?"

"Karate trophies."

"Nifty oak gun cabinet?"

"Oak veneer. I'm on a policeman's salary, gypsy."

"Moosehead mounted on the wall?"

"Give me a little credit, please." She was wearing that smile again, the one that took him by surprise each time he saw it. He knew it was late, that he ought to say good night before she was forced to throw him out, but her smile deserved a few moments of quiet reverence. He had absolutely no resistance against it.

Slowly, holding her in his clear, hypnotic gaze, he raised his hand, brushing the back of his fingers across her cheek. Once. His eyes drifted downward, focusing with dreamy concentration on her lips. He didn't want to frighten her. Feeling as he did, curiosity and desire rioting in his veins, it was probably best that he take things slowly. Hell, who was he kidding? He didn't want to frighten *himself*. This wasn't uncharted territory for him—a man, a woman, and a mutual attraction. And yet... something about this night left him feeling oddly undefended.

"I should go," he said softly. "Thank you for the nursing care, gypsy."

"Oh. You're welcome." Liza stared at him for what seemed to be a very long time. Her thoughts were hazy and unconnected, and when he stood to leave, she could only follow him across the room with her eyes. She put her hand to her cheek, still feeling his touch. She dropped it just as quickly, hoping he hadn't noticed.

He paused in the open doorway, smiling with pure pleasure at the picture she made. A salt-scented breeze whispered through the room, stirring the baby-fine tendrils of hair that framed her face. The blood was warm in her cheeks, and her eyes were overbright. Her mouth was slightly parted, as if she had meant to say something but couldn't quite remember what it was.

"So young," he said softly.

She had no idea why this disturbed her, but it did. "Not so young. I've seen more of this world than most people do in a lifetime."

He liked her. She was so earnest and innocent, a world apart from the faces and personalities he dealt with every day. He stood there, devouring her with his eyes until his resolve began to weaken. Stay or go, stay or . . .

"Good night," Liza said, ending the silent argument.

The corners of his eyes softened with a smile. After a long pause in which he seemed to examine her face, he lifted his hand in a farewell gesture and closed the door softly behind him.

The room seemed unnaturally quiet after Cody had gone. Liza smoothed her skirt with unsteady hands, wishing she could smooth the tension from her body. She could still see him framed in the doorway against the stubborn night, his smile gentling the harsh muscles in his jaw, one lean hip propped against the frame with a lazy grace.

So quiet. She crossed her arms over her chest, the

small movement sending her blouse spilling off one shoulder. Staring straight ahead, her eyes softly unfocused, she ran her palm slowly up her arm, fingers cool and soothing on her bare shoulder. A hesitant smile passed over her mouth.

She liked him.

Chapter

3

"THIS HAS TO be a sin," Liza said to no one in particular.

She was on low simmer beneath a hazy white Mazatlán sun, five feet, four inches of sun-kissed flesh in a black bikini. Her skin was shimmering in perspiration and baby oil, cotton-ball sunspots were dancing behind her closed eyelids, and the surf was whispering in her ear. She was melting into her sand-cushioned beach towel, slowly, slowly...

Tourist noises surrounded her sleepy lethargy. Children shrieking as they ran from the waves that chased them up the beach. Adults murmuring in drowsy monotones. The distant voices of the beach vendors hawking their wares. After a bit of trial and error, Liza had discovered the secret of undisturbed repose on the Mexican beaches. Rather than use the public beach near her cottage and turn away local peddlers every five minutes, she hired a *pulmonia* and traveled to the luxury hotels on the northern shore. Here the tourists were shielded from the peddlers by a vigilant hotel staff and a long white cordon that stretched along the beach. The merchants stood on one side of the rope, waving straw hats and silver jewelry and bright embroidered dresses to catch the rich *turistas'* attention. Should any of the vacationers wish to purchase a souvenir, they crossed the rope into no-man's land and proceeded to bargain. For the most part, the tourists guarded their shiny new sunburns beneath a shady palapa tree, sipping margaritas provided by attentive waiters.

Once or twice in the past, Liza had hired a moped and traveled to a deserted beach several miles out of town. Here the burros outnumbered the tourists, and there was no one to object when she left her swimsuit dangling from the handlebars of the scooter.

More often than not, however, she put on her "tourist" disguise—straw hat, sunglasses, and a dab of zinc oxide on her nose—and strolled through one of the plush hotels as if she owned it. From there it was only a hop, skip, and a jump to the private beach and the icy-cold margaritas. Paradise, compliments of the Camino Real.

The zinc oxide had melted away. Her hat was half-buried in the sand and her sunglasses had disappeared. The sun was beginning its descent in the sky, and the real tourists were shaking off their towels and making plans to meet in the bar or the restaurant. Liza was thoroughly and completely fried. Limp, like a poor flounder washed up on the beach. It was time to roll up the old beach towel and head for home while she still had the energy.

Instead, she fidgeted. She found her sunglasses beneath her towel and polished them to a high gloss. She brushed the sand off her hat and set it neatly beside her. She ordered a Tikki Fruit Fandango and watched the ice cubes melt. The hesitant anticipation she felt melted along with them.

Well, what had she expected? A chance meeting with a green-eyed, dark-haired detective who just *might* be staying at one of the hotels on the north shore?

It would have been nice.

She remembered his touch on her cheek. She had gone to bed the night before still feeling the gentle, almost reverent caress of his hand on her flushed skin. There was something in his eyes, something in his energy and humor that made Cody Davis different from other men. Curiosity, desire, and a strange current of excitement had disturbed Liza's sleep. She was up again at dawn, barely four hours after Cody had left. She told herself she was going to look like hell that night when she performed at the cantina, but she didn't really mind.

Despite her sleepless night, Liza had energy to burn. Thus the decision to play tourist, swimming and sunning, relaxing with an icy margarita. The relentless heat slowly stewed her knotted muscles into milk toast, but Cody's startling impact on her senses remained. She was still humming inside, filled with vague questions and that stubborn, strange excitement. And a quiet disappointment, when a water color sunset spread a halo over the horizon and she accepted the fact that she wouldn't see him that day.

She packed her things in her straw bag—the towel, the baby oil, the Chapstick, and the sunglasses. *I've had a lovely, relaxing day all by myself,* she thought, *and I'm looking forward to singing tonight. I really am. Nothing's changed, nothing at all.*

She almost believed it.

Cody had thrown away his sling that morning, tossing it from the sixth-floor balcony of the Camino Real. His aim was magnificent. It fluttered through the air like a wounded pigeon, sinking quietly into the shallow end of the swimming pool. Today was going to be extraordinary, because Cody willed it so, and he didn't want to be encumbered by the damn sling. Besides, it was giving him heat rash.

Before leaving the hotel, he telephoned Liza's father with his snitch report. Dr. Carlisle was in emergency surgery, but the answering service promised to relay Cody's message. It was short and sweet: "The wandering gypsy is perfectly safe, perfectly healthy, perfectly perfect. More details later. I lost my sling, but will persevere in the face of adversity."

It was still early. Cody killed a couple of hours wandering through the Golden Zone, Mazatlán's unique open-air mall offering local crafts and souvenirs. He made one purchase, a stuffed frog wearing a sombrero and Bermuda shorts. A little conversation piece for Captain Tidwell's desk back at headquarters.

It was nearly ten o'clock when he knocked on Liza's door. He had a bottle of wine in one hand and a beach blanket in the other. The stuffed frog was wrapped in brown butcher paper and tucked beneath his arm. The stitches in his shoulder were throbbing in time with his heartbeat. He hardly noticed. He was preoccupied with the chance he was taking. Liza didn't have a telephone, or he would have called. He had no idea if she had plans for today, or if she even wanted to see him again. He could only go by instinct, and instinct told him to press ahead. A sudden vicious cramp in his shoulder reminded him that his instincts had not always been one hundred percent accurate.

He knocked again, and this time the door slipped its latch and swung wide. Cody called her name, hearing his voice bounce off the empty walls. No answer. No Liza.

From that point on, the day proceeded with uninspiring monotony. Cody spent the afternoon on the beach below Liza's cottage, fending off the local peddlers who traveled the shoreline like a four-lane highway. He drank warm wine and helped a towheaded toddler with a peeling nose build a sand castle. His pulse thumped in odd rhythms whenever he caught sight of a woman who resembled Liza. A chance encounter would have been nice. Hell, a distant glimpse of her would have been nice.

Eventually, a stinging sunburn and a persistent serape peddler drove him from the beach. He made a detour by her cottage, staring at the darkened windows in the fading daylight. The heavy silence was broken only by the sleepy murmur of the ocean.

Unbidden, his mind gave him the luminous texture of her skin, the bewitching curve of her smile, the aristocratic facial bones, and the sweet fragrance of her hair. He wondered where she was.

Liza. The tautness in his body was becoming uncomfortably familiar.

The last request of the evening came from a sonorous, disembodied male voice in a smoky corner of the cantina.

"Would you sing 'Feelings,' for me, sweetheart?"

Liza winced inwardly. "I'm not really familiar with that—"

"Please-oh-please," the voice bounced back. "It's my birthday."

Fortunately, the majority of the patrons in the cantina were feeling no pain. They smiled with misty eyes through Liza's halfhearted rendition of "Feelings," determined to *enjoy*. In fact, Liza received a standing ovation from those who could still stand.

As she left the blinding glare of the spotlight, Liza's curiosity led her gaze to the cottony shadows in search of the birthday boy. She could just imagine the sort of man who would request...

She might have known. It was Miller. He sat grinning in a wreath of cigarette smoke, beckoning with a graceful hand. On his left sat a stunning young woman in a revealing lace halter-dress. And on his right...

On his right sat a dark-haired, green-eyed detective with a grim smile and a freshly sunburned face.

Liza thought she might have stepped off the stage and into a dream. She blinked, but the odd trio was still there. Cody, Miller, and...the Chantilly nymphet.

Slowly, she made her way toward them, trying to

read the message in Cody's eyes. Frustration. A reluctant amusement. And something more, a welcoming light that Liza thought might be reflected in her own eyes.

"Isn't this a surprise?" she said, wondering if she looked as bewildered as she felt. "Are birthday wishes in order, Miller?"

"I lied," Miller confessed. "I don't have birthdays anymore. I just wanted to hear that unforgettable song. Liza, I'd like you to meet my beloved wife, Rebecca."

Liza looked from Miller to Rebecca to Cody. Cody sighed and passed his hand over his eyes.

"Nice to meet you," Liza said blankly. Rebecca giggled, her silver and gold bracelets jangling as they shook hands. "Miller, you never mentioned you were—"

"Married?" Miller shook back his wild mane of hair, his teak-brown face brimming with good humor. "Sweet Liza, I'm every bit as married as you and the Lone Ranger here. Isn't that right, Davis?"

"Miller's been talking to a couple of the waitresses here," Cody said dispiritedly. "And Miller's very thorough."

Rebecca giggled again, running her fingers through her copper curls. "We're not married. I only met him this morning. You're such a tease, Miller."

Miller grinned. "I'm such a tease."

Liza met Cody's heavy-lidded gaze across the table. She opened her eyes wide in mute inquiry.

"Don't look at *me*," Cody said. "Ten minutes ago I was sitting alone at this table. The next thing I know,

Miller's sharing my tequila, and Rebecca is reading my palm."

"And since the fates have thrown the four of us together," Miller added with a wave of said tequila bottle, "and we've straightened out the little misunderstanding of who is not married to whom, I believe we should celebrate. Liza, have you eaten?"

"I usually don't eat dinner when I—"

"Juan's Cantina is very nice," Miller went on thoughtfully, "but a little tame for my taste. I know an excellent nightclub with a mariachi band you won't believe. Pancho's Chew-Choo—have you heard of it? No? Trust me, then. I won't lead you astray. Besides, it will give us all a chance to know each other better."

Cody had spent the entire day with a stuffed frog for company. At this point, he would have gladly sold his soul to the devil to spend five minutes basking in Liza's smile. If Miller and Rebecca were part of the package—and it appeared they were—then so be it. Beggars could not be choosers.

"Sounds good to me," he said. "Liza? Are you in the mood for mariachis?"

Liza was not. She wanted to take Cody's hand and lead him into the luscious night. She wanted to kick off her shoes and run barefoot along the beach. She wanted to flop full-length on the sand and count every star in the sky. She wanted to see the moonlight pick out the tiny smile lines at the corners of Cody's eyes. Her gaze meshed with his, the silent exchange crackling with an intuitive understanding.

Her chest lifted with a sigh. "Lead the way."

They took two separate *pulmonias*. Somehow

Miller managed to squeeze in beside Liza, while Rebecca and Cody followed behind. The night was balmy and rich with starlight. Liza kept looking over her shoulder, feeling melancholy. Obviously, fate had it in for her today.

Pancho's Chew-Choo offered international cuisine and live music in a funky thatched-roof cabana under Ice Box Hill. Roaming mariachi and marimba bands made quiet conversation almost impossible. Liza picked halfheartedly at her food, acutely conscious of Cody sitting next to her at the table. His sling was gone, but she hadn't had a chance to ask him about it. He was wearing pleated khaki trousers and a baby-blue cotton shirt. His bruises were nicely disguised behind his sunburn. Since arriving at the restaurant, he had assumed that objective look of his, the one that disguised his thoughts from the world. He might have been thinking about the seascape hanging on the wall, or the guacamole dip. He was a blank page.

Liza's breath caught sharply in her throat when she felt his hand on her thigh beneath the table. Her skirt was made of whisper-thin gauze, and she could feel the heat of his palm through the material. He was looking at Miller, apparently absorbed in the conversation that had sprung up during a lull in the music. Miller was making his point with exaggerated gestures, creating pictures with every word. Rebecca was fishing a corn chip out of the salsa, ducking to avoid Miller's long arms.

Cody's hand moved slightly, fingers spreading over the soft white gauze. Liza was taken completely unaware by the surge of warm blood that ran through the secret depths of her body. She stirred fitfully, her hand covering the pulse that jumped in her throat.

"Your face looks a little flushed above your cheekbones," Rebecca commented. Rebecca had aspirations of becoming a personal beauty consultant, and professsed herself acutely sensitive to "nature's color wheel." "You know, you might consider using a blush with more of a bronze base. The peach tone you have on now turns a bit orange on your complexion. I hope you don't mind constructive criticism?"

"What? Oh... of course not." Liza took a deep breath. "It's rather warm in here, don't you think?"

Cody stood up abruptly, pushing his chair back with a clatter. "Time to go," he said briskly, catching Liza's hand and pulling her to her feet. "Rebecca, it was very nice meeting you. I hate to run out on your party, Miller, but Liza and I have an early morning tomorrow. We're going fishing."

"We are?" Liza asked blankly.

"We are. Mazatlán is the billfish capital of the world, Liza. I'm surprised you don't know that."

"*Bull*fish, did you say?" Miller murmured, arching one golden brow.

"Billfish," Cody repeated laconically. "I wish you the best of luck at beauty school, Rebecca. I'm sure you'll do well. Miller, if we don't run into you again, have a pleasant vacation."

"Oh, I'll be around a while yet," Miller said cheerfully. "'She is a woman, therefore to be wooed; She is a woman, therefore may be won.'"

"I like that," Rebecca said, diverted. "Miller, was that a poem or something?"

"Shakespeare," Miller said affably, holding Cody's

gaze. "*Titus Andronicus*. A damn fine piece of writing. Are you sure you two can't stay and have dessert? They make a mango fruit sundae here that's out of this world."

"Another time," Cody said. His smile fought with the tense muscles in his jaw. Miller O'Keefe was a nuisance that could be dealt with later. For now, Cody's driving impulse was to eliminate the distance between Liza and himself. Throughout the evening he had felt his perceptions narrowing, focusing with acute clarity on every move she made, every word she spoke, the tangled fall of her hair, and the sweet, unusual huskiness of her voice. When she had performed tonight, Cody had been blessedly anonymous in the shadows of the smoky room. There were no games to play then, no pretenses to keep up. Simply looking at her had brought him pleasure beyond imagination. And all the while desire had remained with him, lingering in his heart and mind like the tantalizing fragrance of her perfume...

Miller sighed and stood up, bowing over Liza's free hand. "Thank you for my song, sweet Liza."

Cody didn't like Miller kissing her hand. The gesture smacked of pretension. He felt entirely justified in whisking Liza away from him and out the door before she could blink.

Outside, the night sky sparkled above them like a dazzling jewel. Night winds carried the salty tang of the sea and the faint aroma of exhaust from the idling taxis. Cody waved away the eager drivers who converged on them. Liza watched him, hands on her hips, Bambi browns glittering with a dangerous light.

"What do you think you're doing?" she asked softly. Too softly.

"I thought we'd walk," Cody said.

"Where to?"

"I don't know."

Their eyes locked. Liza stood stock-still on the steps leading from the restaurant, trying to sort out her storm-tossed thoughts. Cody stood on the cobblestone drive below her, hands pushed deep in his pockets, eyes brighter than smoldering embers.

"I might have wanted to stay," Liza said when he didn't speak.

"Did you?"

"You could have asked."

"I didn't need to."

Liza knew he spoke the simple truth. She could accept it or ignore it. Thanks to Jeremy, a bruised corner of her spirit still flinched when she experienced even the most inconsequential loss of control. Still tangled in his gaze, she tried to grasp her anger and hold it. It was futile. Not while he looked at her with those beautiful, brooding eyes . . .

He waited, tension shimmering over his features. After a long moment, Liza walked down to him, silently holding out her hand. She was shaky inside, but the doubts were intertwined with inevitability. What would happen would happen. Her will was spilling like sand through her fingers.

"It's a long walk home," she said huskily, shivering when he threaded his fingers through hers. Her flesh stung, and all from the touch of his hand . . .

What would it be like when he held her? Suddenly, she wanted it so much, the level of her heedlessness frightened her. *Beware of what you want—you just may get it*. Book of Jeremy, chapter one, verse one.

"I realize it's a long walk," Cody said, tugging gently on her hand. "And I've earned every minute of it."

Hand in hand, they followed the narrow strip of asphalt that curved, dipped, and twisted down to the bay. Now and again they were forced to stand in the soft earth at the side of the road while a taxi bounced past them. The moonlight was lavish on the quiet hillside, the long grass tickled Liza's knees, and the warm, sweet scent of flowers enveloped them. Cody used words sparingly. Occasionally, he would murmur something witty and utterly charming, such as, "Mind your step." Frustration was eating him alive. She was enticingly near, her hand warm and soft in his, her silhouette etched in starlight against the night. He tried desperately to think of things that would keep his mind off her. This was neither the time nor the place to give in to the desire that was wreaking havoc with his peace of mind. There were taxis to dodge. There were tourists to mingle among. And there was this bloody awkward silence to deal with.

What are you thinking, Liza?

They came to a crossroads, the ocean shimmering in front of them, Avenida Olas Atlas stretching to either side. More taxis. More tourists. An explosion of light and sound. Cody turned south, toward Liza's cottage. By now he had made a mental list of places on her face and body he couldn't trust himself to look at.

"Not that way," Liza said suddenly. "I know a shortcut. Follow me." Before Cody could respond, she darted across the avenue, a wraithlike figure in a papery white dress. *Pulmonias* zipped happily past her, wind-whipping her skirt to her thighs. A sensual response shivered through Cody's nerves as he stared at the bright-haired siren smiling across the way. He wondered if she realized what devastating power her smile wielded. Never once had he seen her use her breathtaking looks as a weapon, and it amazed him. Perhaps Liza scorned mirrors as she did plants.

He caught up with her on the wide cobblestone walkway that separated Avenida Olas Atlas from the steep embankment that led to the ocean. She was leaning over the white concrete wall, her features reflecting the shimmer of moonlight on water. He stood next to her, watching her like a starving man at a feast. The stars had drifted from the sky, glittering in her hair. The wind from the sea teased the fabric of her skirt, pulling it taut against her legs. Her eyes were fixed on the water with a child's dreamy, unblinking stare. He wanted to say the right thing to her, but the words escaped him.

"It's beautiful here," Liza said quietly. "Don't you think? Like something out of a storybook."

I've never seen anything so beautiful in my life. "Is this the shortcut you mentioned?"

Liza's smile was whimsical and restless. "Yes."

His dark, sparkling gaze met hers, taking on the faintest hint of amusement. "We're swimming you home, then?"

"I said it was a shortcut. I never said it led to the

cottage." If there was a more discreet way of doing this, Liza didn't know it. She tried to calm her fluttering heart with deep, even breaths.

Cody didn't move. Very softly, he said, "Then where does it lead?"

It's your move, Gloria Steinem, Liza told herself. And before she could think, not *daring* to think, she whispered, "I don't want to wait any longer. I'm no good at waiting. Couldn't you just . . . hold me?"

Cody released a short, shaken breath. For a moment, he was lost in a quiet storm of emotions, helpless against the suspended sexual longing in her eyes. His hands lifted slowly to frame either side of her face. His fingers were trembling, and the flesh beneath his palms felt feverish.

"I was only waiting to be asked," he said. His smile was soft and new, touching her heart.

The wind blew her hair around him like a garland. Her hands were on his chest, absorbing the hard drumming of his heart. Inches separated their faces, then only a breath. His lips parted softly, his gaze narrowed and intense. His mouth closed over hers with dreamy eroticism, a gentle, featherlight caress that imparted deep-rooted sensations. His fingers whispered over her face, stroking the delicate hollows and sensitive curves. He pulled back slightly, a hard flush staining his cheeks, then his mouth maneuvered over her lips again, back and forth in an urgent, barely restrained rhythm that left her aching and unbearably aroused.

Cody lifted his head. Below him, her eyes were liquid gold, sleepy with passion. He put his fingers against her lips, a gentle pressure. "I know a short-cut," he said huskily. "Follow me."

He vaulted the low retaining wall, then placed his hands on Liza's waist and lifted her over the concrete barrier. The stitches in his shoulder burned in fury, promising retribution. Cody was oblivious to the pain.

Hand in hand, they ran with childish abandon down the sandy hillock to the beach. They were alone there, alone with the gentle starlight and the misty winds off the ocean. Above and beyond, the sights and sounds of Mazatlán faded to a dream.

There was no time for hesitation. Time had suddenly become something infinitely precious to Cody. She was in his arms, her soft curves pressed hard against him. With the stars swirling around them and the moist air glazing their skin, they kissed, desperate, urgent kisses that fed a growing hunger. He kissed her eyes, her mouth, her hair; he licked at the warm fragrant skin of her neck and nuzzled the sensitive folds of her ear. He couldn't get close enough. He couldn't have enough.

Liza was burning, burning... every inch of her flesh was begging for his touch. She gasped with pleasure when his hands moved to her breasts, kneading the heavy, aching warmth. Her nipples thrust against his palms, and she heard the pleasure sounds deep in his throat. She could feel the hard length of him as he kissed her, the hungry pressure of his hips moving against her. Desire spilled like molten lava through her body...

Too strong. Powerful enough to turn Liza inside-out with longing, powerful enough to shatter every thread of her control. Suddenly, mingling with the demands of her body came a sensation of danger. She pulled away, breathing as though there were no oxygen in the air.

"What is it?" Cody's eyes were softly unfocused, glazed with passion. He could still taste her.

"I can't." Liza's throat was dry and aching.

"Why?"

How could she explain what she barely understood herself? "It's all happening so fast. I'm afraid."

Cody smoothed his hand over her hair, holding her face in a tender, exploring gaze. "Of me?"

"No." Whatever else happened, she couldn't allow him to think that. "I think . . . I'm afraid I'll lose myself." A shadow of a smile. "You can do that taking shortcuts."

Cody waited until he was sure he had himself under control. Then he placed a kiss on her forehead, a touch so gentle Liza thought she might have imagined it. "We may have a little problem here. Patience isn't my strong suit, gypsy."

"I don't know what I'm going to do," Liza whispered. "This is crazy."

"Good crazy?" he asked, his hands weaving gentle patterns up and down her arms.

Her eyes remained solemn, shadowed. "Very good."

He sighed, resting his forehead against hers. Her hair, smelling like strawberries, tickled his cheek, surrounded him in silk. "What do you want from me, then?"

Waves of sensation continued to ripple through her even now. She closed her eyes briefly, fighting the urge to cover his face with kisses. *Dammit Liza, is you or is you ain't?* "I think I want time."

"Try to say that with a little more conviction, would you? For the sake of my sanity, if nothing else."

"Time," she whispered to his chin.

The edges of his smile were slightly frayed. "Then I think I'd better take you home, gypsy. Only to the front door, of course. Unless you'd like me to stay with . . . no. No, don't answer that. I didn't mean it."

"All things considered"—she took a sharp breath as his lips tickled the pulse in her throat—"I think I'll see myself home."

A moment of heavy silence passed before he asked softly, "Are you sure?"

She pulled away from the shelter of his arms, blinking the ocean mist off her lashes. Pleasure tears. "I'm sure. Cody?"

His arms felt empty. "What?"

"I wasn't expecting you," she said helplessly. "I wasn't expecting *this*. I don't have my fences up."

"Is that so terrible?"

"No. Yes."

Cody nodded. "I'm glad we cleared that up. Tell me something, gypsy."

She looked away from him, turning her face into the wind. "What?"

"These fences of yours . . . just what are they supposed to protect you from?"

The million-dollar question, put with charming and deceptive simplicity. Liza stared blindly over the ocean, looping her hair behind her ears in a childish, vulnerable gesture.

"Myself," she whispered.

She left him without another word, running up the embankment to the road. Cody's eyes followed her every step of the way.

Chapter
4

THERE WAS A fine art to a bubble bath.

First and foremost one should have quality bubbles. No cheap pink powders that smelled like Tinkerbell cologne and left a rainbow soap scum. The key word here was *money*. The more you spent, the sweeter your bubble bath smelled, and the longer your bubbles would last. Liza had invested heavily in bath crystals. They were displayed in clear glass canisters in the windowsill above her antique claw-foot tub. She had a variety of colors and scents, from a lively Christmas Evergreen to a sensual Midnight Musk. Best of all, a tiny capful of these sparkling crystals produced creamy mountains of bubbles that would last forever. A must for the ever-popular bubble sculpture.

Music was also a necessity. Liza enjoyed classical guitar for a relaxing evening soak and old-fashioned, "get-down" sixties music for the morning splash. The occasional midnight bubble binge was always underscored by sweet jazz with mellow sax.

Naturally, certain types of snacks accompanied certain types of music. The classical guitar cried out for corn chips and salsa, or perhaps a steaming cup of Mexican chocolate. Buffalo Springfield was far more enjoyable with a peanut-butter-and-banana sandwich in hand. The versatile Snickers bar seemed to go well with everything.

Yes, indeed . . . there was a fine art to a bubble bath, and Liza Carlisle had a degree in fine art.

This particular morning, for instance, called for the pale green crystals labeled "Tropical Rainfall." Liza was feeling a little out of sorts, and the fresh, clean fragrance was just the thing to perk up her spirits. A nice healthy glass of pineapple juice stood by on the side of the tub, and Buffalo Springfield was blasting from the tape player atop the toilet tank.

If she had to label her little depression, she would call it "Cody Junior." He hadn't called . . . which in all fairness was understandable, since she had no phone. Neither had he stopped by the cottage to visit, or dropped in at the cantina to hear her sing. The promised fishing trip had never materialized. The billfish or bullfish or whatever the heck they were called were still alive and well, swimming off the coast of Mazatlán.

As far as she knew. Cody himself had told her he wasn't a patient man. There were probably any number of tourist-type lovelies willing to help him reel in a whopper. Liza sighed and patted a bubble-beard on her face.

"Did I or did I not tell you to lock your door?"

Liza gasped, inhaling a frothy spray of Tropical Rainfall. She sneezed several times in succession, her watery eyes trying to bring the tall figure in the bathroom doorway into focus. *"Cody?"*

"In the flesh," he said. "And speaking of which, you look very nice in a beard and a birthday suit. I wish I'd brought my camera."

He was wearing well-washed blue jeans, a white baseball cap, and a loud Hawaiian shirt. He carried a little green plant in a miniature clay pot, festively decorated with a red satin ribbon.

"You scared me to death!" Liza slumped to her chin in the water, sending a bubble-wave surging over the side of the tub. "You can't just walk in here!"

"Anyone can walk in here," Cody said mildly. "That's my whole point. Lock your door and you won't have evil-minded voyeurs wandering through your bathroom." He raised the potted plant with a bright smile. "I brought you a present, gypsy. It's high time you made a commitment to some greenery."

"Will you get out of here?"

"I can't hear you, the music's too loud." Cody walked over to the tape player and flicked it off. "That's better. You know, I did knock. I could hear the music playing—the entire coastline could hear the music playing—but you didn't answer, so I thought I'd check up on you. Where would you like your plant?"

Liza groaned in her bubbles. "Kitchen."

"I thought it would look kind of nice in here." Cody rested one hip against the sink, taking in his surroundings with a lively, exploring gaze. He noted the bath crystals crowding the windowsill, the soft braided rug on the floor, the delicate watercolor hanging on the wall. "This is fascinating," he said conversationally. "You've made your little nest in the bathroom. The rest of the cottage looks completely barren. It's almost as if you don't want anyone to know you might feel at home here."

The temperature in the bath was dropping rapidly. Liza shivered in her chicken-skinned flesh. "I'm not holding an open house in here, Detective. I'm taking a bath. With your remarkable powers of observation, I'm surprised that escaped your notice."

"Now she's getting testy." Cody pushed his hat back on his head, a wicked smile teasing the corners of his eyes. "Aren't you going to ask me where I've been the past couple of days?"

Even expensive bubbles dissipated sooner or later. "Not now. Go away."

"My shoulder was giving me fits." He set the plant carefully on the edge of the sink. "I've been laying low in my hotel room since Friday night."

Now Liza saw what she had missed before. His cheeks were stained with fever colors, his skin dry and taut. The faintest shimmer of perspiration glittered on his forehead. Laying low in his hotel room . . . what did that mean? Unconscious? Hallucinating? Flirting with death? With these *mucho macho* types, one never knew. "Are you all right, Cody?"

"Fine." His smile spread slowly beneath over-bright eyes. "You look adorable in bubbles. May I come in?" Cody asked.

Liza reached for a towel, trying to keep everything vital submerged. "You have a way of ruining a beautiful bubble bath. Why don't you lie down on the—damn, I can't reach it—lie down on the couch, while I dress?"

He handed her the towel, making a great show of keeping his eyes averted. "I don't want to lie down. I've been flat on my back for two days. This is amazing. It smells like a jungle in here." He paused, then added thoughtfully, "And it's raining."

"I'm not getting out of here until you leave," Liza said gently. "Do you want to be responsible for me catching pneumonia?"

Somewhere in the back of his mind, Cody faced the possibility he wasn't being entirely rational. On the heels of this realization came another, even less pleasant suspicion—he was making a bloody fool of himself. He sighed, rubbing his throbbing shoulder. "Do you have any Tylenol around?"

"In the kitchen, in the cabinet above the sink."

She looked so soft and warm and luscious with her knees drawn up to her chin and the bubbles floating in little islands around her. The upper curves of her breasts were shimmering with the most incredible shade of pink. Her hair was a tangled, sun-colored cloud on the top of her head, one water-darkened curl curving in a question mark over her shoulder. Her nose was dotted with a smear of bubbles at the tip.

A fever gave a man excuses to do the most outrageous things.

"I'll go find the pills," he promised, "very soon now."

He knelt beside the tub in one fluid motion, tak-

ing her chin in his hand and drawing her toward him
with gentle force. His lips met hers with the fever's
heat between them, caressing, demanding, teasing.
Liza responded in spite of herself, in spite of the rapidly cooling water and disappearing bubbles and the
suspicion that she was kissing a fevered lunatic. His
hands were tangled in her hair, urging her closer.
Liza was mesmerized by the exquisite, dragging
pressure of his lips, then almost frantic. She broke
from him, arms crossed against her breasts, her
breath coming in jarring inhalations.

"Yes?" he whispered thickly.

"No." The word was a ragged sigh.

Glittering droplets of water rolled slowly between
the lush curves of her breasts. Cody wanted to lick
them away, one by one . . .

"I'm running amok, aren't I?" he asked.

"Completely."

"I thought so." For the first time he noticed that
his hat was floating in the water. He picked it up
carefully, his thumb skimming the curve of Liza's
thigh. "Tylenol," he said.

She looked at him through a wave of tension. "Tylenol."

Dripping hat in hand, he rose and walked slowly
out of the room. Liza followed him with her eyes,
sinking lower and lower into a chilly jungle rainfall . . .

"Take off your shirt," she said.

It wasn't the first time she had asked him. Immediately after dressing in shorts and knit shirt, she had
discovered him sitting on her kitchen counter,

swearing at the child-proof cap on the Tylenol bottle. The heat from his body burned the air between them. Liza gave him the pills and a cool glass of bottled water, then asked to see his shoulder. Macho Detective Davis had patted her on the head and told her to mellow out.

She'd fixed him a sandwich that had gone untouched. She offered to take him to the doctor and was rewarded with a dimpled smile and another pat on the head. Now Cody was sprawled on her sofa, verbally planning a sightseeing tour for that very afternoon.

"We could rent a jeep and drive to Copala," he said. "It's an old mining pueblo dating back to the conquistadores. The desk clerk at the hotel said it was a must."

"Maybe you didn't hear me." Liza settled herself next to him on the sofa, preparing for battle. "I asked you to take off your shirt."

His smile was a luxuriant, fevered haze. "Too late. You had your chance in the bathroom. What do you say to Copala?"

"I say"—Liza probed the buttons of his shirt with a sweet smile— "take this off."

"You're a wanton and unprincipled woman, and your mother would be ashamed of you."

"Off. I want to see that wound. If it wasn't infected, you wouldn't be feverish."

"It's just fine," Cody said soothingly. "A little sore, maybe, but that's my own fault. I should have been wearing my sling."

"Then why aren't you?"

"I threw it in the swimming pool."

Liza's fingers curled tightly into fists. "Of course you did. I don't know why that surprises me. Now do you think you could get out of your Charlie Bronson mode long enough for me to look at that shoulder?"

She wasn't going to let it go. Cody knew precisely what his shoulder looked like, and it wasn't pretty. He also knew a determined woman when he saw one. His mouth quirked at the corner, doubting the wisdom of his action even as he shrugged out of his shirt. "All right. But please remember I've been through this kind of thing once or twice before, and I know when to worry. The last two days in my hotel room, when my fever was so high I saw pink iguanas, I worried. This morning I woke up feeling ninety-nine percent better. The worst is over."

She wasn't listening. She was staring at the puckered mound of fiery flesh beneath his collarbone, horrified by the angry streaks of infection. "Why didn't you call me?"

"You don't have a phone," he reminded her kindly.

"You shouldn't have been alone." She placed her hand gently near the wound, flinching when she felt the throbbing heat beneath her palm. "Cody, are you sure you shouldn't see a doctor? Or what about some hydrogen peroxide? I could soak the wound in—"

"Scratch that idea," Cody said firmly. "No hydrogen peroxide, Florence Nightingale. I told you, I'm feeling much better. I'm still taking the antibiotics they gave me in the hospital."

Desperate to offer some sort of comfort, Liza awkwardly smoothed the tangled hair from his forehead. It was that or take his pulse. "You're sure?"

"Sure," he said, his eyes glittering with a soft light that sent warning signals through her body. She broke away from his gaze with some effort, her eyes traveling slowly down the hard musculature of his chest. The taut expanse of naked flesh looked beautiful to her, bone and muscle knit into intoxicating ridges and hollows. And like a chipped sculpture of Michelangelo's *David*, the pure, masculine lines of his body had their flaws. An old scar was partially visible above his low-slung jeans, cutting diagonally across his abdomen. A cloudy purple bruise marred the sweet play of skin stretching across his ribs. Bright pink tissue tucked a doughnut-shaped scar on the shoulder Liza had gotten used to thinking of as his "good" shoulder. Apparently, Cody didn't have a good shoulder.

"You *have* been through this once or twice before," she said faintly.

He leaned his head back against the sofa, his long length relaxed, the wide mouth breathtakingly sensual. "I'm really not as dangerous as I look. One of these beauties came from a humdrum appendectomy."

Watching him, Liza felt a stab of pure longing so powerful it made her stomach hurt. "And other than that," she said with forced lightness, "you're a regular Clint Eastwood clone, all granite and steel."

"I have my weaknesses, believe me." Wry amusement tinged his voice. "Ordinary human foibles. I turn green in an airplane. I can't sleep during a thunderstorm. My shoulder holster has ruined every shirt I own. Have you ever seen Clint Eastwood's shoulder holster bleed on his shirts?"

"No," Liza said thoughtfully. "Then you're just a man, after all?"

For a long, quiet moment, he held her wantonly beautiful gaze. "Disappointed?"

The rich color of her cheeks framed a bewitching smile. "Nah. I like wimps."

Sunbeams poured over them like cream from the narrow-arched windows, so warm, so gentle. They sat and looked at each other, with amusement for a time, then with a subtle, growing tension. Their smiles fell away slowly, first Cody's, then Liza's. She wanted to touch him. Her trembling fingers spread over his chest, and she heard the breath catch in his throat. She felt the startling strength beneath the bone and sinew, her hands drifting over the sun-kissed flesh. She moved closer, nuzzling her cheek against his chest, inhaling the sweet, musky fragrance of his skin.

"I just wanted to feel you," she whispered.

Moving with a dreamy sensuality, Cody's hands framed her face for his kiss. Warm and lazy, their mouths moved against each other's, tasting, touching, tempting. Rocking together, until her mouth was deeply open to him and she was breathing in quick, shallow inhalations. Her thighs tightened instinctively when he slipped his hand beneath her shirt to mold the underside of her breast, pressing upward on the aching heaviness.

"What was that?" Cody whispered against her mouth.

She caught his lower lip between her teeth, tugging gently. "What was what?"

"That sound. Did you hear—"

Liza heard. A heavy knocking on her door, a special knock used by only one person. *Shave and a haircut . . . two bits.*

"Juan," she groaned. "It's Juan. I forgot he was coming to pick me up."

She was off Cody's lap in a flash, into the bathroom, back again tugging a brush through her hair. Cody was precisely where she had left him, staring at the door with brooding eyes.

"I don't like him," he said. "Who is he?"

"Juan Rivera. He owns the cantina. I always help him with his bookkeeping on Mondays." Another knock. "Don't you want to put your shirt on?"

"I don't know where it is."

She found his shirt on the floor behind the couch. Cody was still buttoning it when the front door swung wide. George Hamilton—or his Mexican twin—was framed against the white sunlight, an elegant figure in beige cotton slacks and an ice-blue shirt.

"You never lock it, *querida*," Juan announced sadly. "I have installed for you this wonderful dead-bolt lock, and do you use it? Not once."

Cody felt the tension building at the base of his neck. He stood slowly, studying Juan Rivera with fire-bright eyes. Obviously a good friend, if he felt free to walk in her home unannounced. Considerate, if he was indeed responsible for installing the dead bolt. Good old Juan.

"I lost the key," Liza said. "I told you I would, I can never hang on to keys. Juan, I'd like you to meet Cody Davis, a friend of mine from Colorado."

Cody followed the rules of polite conversation. He

shook hands. He asked about Juan's family, his business, his home in Mazatlán. He brushed off Juan's suggestion that Liza stay and visit with her friend from Colorado rather than going in to work.

"I'll be here for another week," Cody said smoothly. "We'll have plenty of time together."

"*You* may be here," Juan said, "but one never knows about Liza. Just last week she was talking about visiting the Mayan ruins in Cancun. Each day I expect to find a note telling me she has gone."

Cody smiled coolly. "You have a reputation, Liza. Your wanderlust is catching up with you."

"Oh, I've reformed," Liza said promptly. "I'm a homebody now. I own a plant."

"Yes?" Juan murmured, eyebrows raised in polite inquiry. "A cactus that does not require much attention, perhaps? Or a lifelike plastic fern?"

"I won't even dignify that remark with a reply." Liza turned to Cody, laying her fingers on his arm. "I won't be long. Will you stay and take care of my plant?"

It might have been the fever. There was an insulated pain deep inside his skull that the Tylenol had no effect on. It might have been the physical yearning that gave him no peace. It might have been the gloomy outlook for the last unbroken heart in Denver, Colorado. Jealousy was spinning a nasty little web around his cheerful indifference.

For whatever reason, Cody decided to be difficult.

"I think I'll take that trip to Copala," he said.

"You can't do that," Liza protested. "You're still weak. You should be resting."

What with one thing and another, Cody's traitorous knees suddenly gave notice. He dropped abruptly to the sofa, feeling brand-new nerve chills rattling his skin. "I'm fine," he said. Charlie Bronson would have been proud. "Just fine. I'm looking forward to Copala. Juan, have you any idea where I could rent a jeep?"

Juan exchanged speaking glances with Liza. "I'm not certain... possibly Hotel Playa Mazatlán. Mr. Davis, if you've been ill, you might want to postpone your trip. The road to Copala is difficult at best, a dirt track through mountainous terrain. There are storm warnings out for this evening, particularly the eastern provinces."

"I'm from Colorado," Cody said. He closed his eyes briefly against the demon headache. "I can drive through anything."

Liza had been watching his face closely. "You know you're not well, Cody. Please stay here until I get back, and then we can—"

"I don't need a baby-sitter," Cody interrupted. "Please, just go with Juan. We've already delayed him long enough. I'll give your new plant a nice drink of water and grab a taxi to Hotel Playa Mazatlán. No problem."

"I really wish you wouldn't—"

"If wishes were booze, we could party for a year." His smile was brilliant, blood-hot skin stretched tight over stark cheekbones. He wondered with an odd detachment if he looked as disoriented as he felt. "Go to work, Liza."

She took a hard breath. Juan murmured something about waiting in the car and left. Silence spread, settling heavily in the deep, shadowed

corners of the room. When was the last time she had
been able to look at him without her heart jumping
into her throat?

"Stubborn," she said.

Wanting her, striving for lightness, he said, "Who,
me? I'm a pussycat, gypsy."

"You're really going to Copala?"

"Why not?"

"*Why not?*" Liza snapped. His baseball cap was
balanced on the arm of the sofa. She picked it up,
fitting it none too gently on his head. "Have a nice
trip, Charlie."

She left, slamming the door behind her in the
grand tradition.

Chapter

5

"CODY JUNIOR," that niggling little depression, was rapidly becoming "Cody Senior." Liza worked like a Trojan in Juan's office at the cantina until six o'clock that evening and accomplished absolutely nothing. Her imagination was eating her alive.

Cody is driving through the jungle in a khaki-green jeep with a jaunty little fringed top. He's perspiring heavily. His shoulder is throbbing. Fresh bloodstains are seeping through his flowered shirt. So much blood . . .

He begins to get light-headed, dizzy, disoriented. Where is he? Hawaii? Aspen? His fever returns, and he hallucinates. He runs the jeep smack into a palm tree that looks like a garage. His last conscious thought is of Liza . . .

Finally, Liza abandoned the books and ledgers and walked out of the cantina into a steady curtain of rain. The fair-weather *pulmonias* had vanished. Taxis were few and far between, and crammed with dripping tourists. Liza walked for fifteen minutes before Juan's silver-blue Mercedes pulled up alongside and the door swung open.

"If you'll recall, I was going to take you to dinner after work." Juan sighed. "Looking as you do, that is no longer an option. Get in."

Liza pushed the dripping bangs out of her eyes with her fist. "I'll ruin your upholstery, Juan. I'm drenched."

"I realized that when I saw you scurrying along the boulevard like a drowned rat. The fact that I stopped says a great deal for our friendship."

Juan was a true gentleman throughout the ride home. Never once did he ask Liza why she had forgotten their dinner date. He carried on an entire conversation by himself, asking and answering his own questions, pointing out the fresh thunderheads moving in from the east. Never once did he ask about Liza's friend with the Hawaiian shirt and the glassy green eyes. Juan's relationship with Liza was purely platonic, based on mutual respect and understanding. Juan was a dedicated bachelor with a passion for one-night stands. He made it a practice never to become involved with someone he truly liked.

The Mercedes rolled to a halt beneath the blinking neon sign of the Golden Palms condominiums. "Can I walk you to your door?" Juan asked, infusing his voice with an overdose of sincerity and enthusiasm.

Liza eyed his immaculate slacks and shirt through her watering mascara. "Are you kidding?"

"Yes, indeed," he said promptly. "Now, before you make a mad dash for your cottage, I would like to ask you a personal question."

"Ask away."

"Is there anything I can do?"

Liza smiled faintly, watching the rain drizzle over the gray-tinted windshield. "Such an observant man."

"*Querida*, you did irreparable damage to my book-keeping system today. I have just spent twenty minutes talking gibberish to a statue. It does not take a genius to know you have something on your mind. Possibly it has something to do with your friend who drove to Copala this afternoon?"

"He wasn't well," Liza said, attempting lightness. "I can't help but be concerned. I just wish I knew he was . . . safe."

"You and he are . . . ?"

"No."

"No?"

Her soft, golden eyes narrowed thoughtfully. "Not yet," she whispered.

The cottage was dark and silent. Liza flicked on one of the brass floor lamps in the living room, then made a beeline for the bathroom. If ever a woman needed the comfort of a soothing bubble bath, tonight was the night.

She stripped off her clothes, dropping them with a

wet slap on the tile floor. Her favorite George Winston tape in the recorder. Peaches and Cream bath crystals. And for food . . .

She padded down the hall to the kitchen, naked as the day she was born. The fridge yielded the perfect "George Winston, Peaches and Cream" snack: Sara Lee cheesecake. After a split second's hesitation, she also grabbed her last bottle of wine cooler—peach flavored.

She soaked and ate and drank. When the tape ran out, she hopped out of the tub and replaced it with Fresh Aire, then hopped back in again. More bath crystals, another infusion of hot water. The muscles that Cody Davis had tied into knots eight hours earlier slowly relaxed. Vowing not to think about him again, she sank deeper and deeper into the steamy water, heavy eyelids drifting closed . . .

Cody has been driving for hours. The fever and disabling chills are back. Suddenly, the dirt track he has been following opens to a muddy riverbank. He slams on his brakes, but the fever has dulled his reflexes. The jeep skids sideways into the river, battered mercilessly to and fro by the foaming rapids. Cody can't swim with his injured arm. The water is closing around him, and his last thought is of . . .

Choking on Peaches and Cream bubbles, Liza fought her way out of the water. She'd nearly drowned in the bathtub, and all because of Detective Davis. What a pathetic state she was in. It was time to call it a night. She gave herself a brisk rubdown with a towel, then used the blow dryer on her hair. A little Oil of Olay for the complexion, and she was off to the bedroom.

She didn't bother with a light. She didn't bother with clothes. She tumbled into bed with a sigh, and then tumbled right out again with a muffled shriek.

The body on the bed stirred, groaned, and subsided into light snores.

Cowering on the floor, clad only in goosebumps, Liza slowly raised her head to peer over the edge of the bed. The image was blurred in the shadows, but clearly masculine. She could barely make out the bold print of a colorful Hawaiian shirt. Either Tom Selleck had dropped in for a visit, or Cody Davis had never left.

She dressed by touch in the darkness, slipping on a white cotton gown and robe. Her hands were trembling. She couldn't decide if she was angry, relieved, or simply frightened half to death. He wasn't lying unconscious in the jungle. He was barely four feet away, cradling her feather pillow and snoring like a baby.

She flipped on the light in the hallway, then stood at the bedroom door and took a deep, sustaining breath. He was stretched out on his back, fully clothed, as if he had intended to lie down for just a moment, then forgotten to get up again. His dark hair was sweetly tumbled, a sharp contrast against the pale pink pillowcase. His mouth was slightly parted, his lashes a soft, spiky shadow against his cheeks.

Quietly, Liza crossed the room, placing her hand lightly on his forehead. No fever. It must have been sheer exhaustion that was making him sleep so soundly. Her hand moved of its own volition, gently smoothing the tangled hair from his brow. He was beautiful in the soft vulnerability of sleep.

She took yet another deep, sustaining breath— and one last glance—and left the room.

It was still dark when the thunder began. Liza was drifting in and out of dreams, fighting the broken spring on the living room sofa. She opened her eyes as a shaft of lightning ripped the sky outside her window, illuminating the room to noonday brightness. She focused on the tall, dark figure standing before the window, both hands spread on the glass that was peppered with rain. The angry shock of answering thunder rattled through the house.

I have my weaknesses . . . I can't sleep during thunderstorms . . .

She sat up on the sofa, knuckling the sleep from her eyes. Cody turned, backlit by another blast of light. There were stones set in his eyes.

"I've put you out of your bed," he said tonelessly. "I'm sorry."

Liza shrugged out of the blanket that had twisted around her hips. "It doesn't matter."

"It does matter." His husky voice seemed to echo in the storm-shrouded room. "I was just going to rest for a minute. I never meant to fall asleep."

"Cody—"

Thunder again, sending an earthquake of sound rattling through the walls. Cody closed his eyes, his hands clenching into fists at his side. "Talk to me, Liza," he whispered. "Be with me. I don't want to think."

It wasn't a time for questions. Acting purely on instinct, Liza crossed the room, slipping her arms around his waist and tucking her head in the hollow of his shoulder. "I don't know what to say. I don't know what to do."

His hand brushed the hair from her temple. His skin was ice-cold. "What did you do today?"

"Nothing. Ordinary things."

"Good. I want to hear about ordinary things. Tell me."

She led him to the couch, tucking the blanket around them both. Rain hit the windows in blasts. The night was a chameleon, alternately black and white, fierce and quiet. Liza nuzzled her face against Cody's chest and told him about her day. The mistakes she had made with payroll. The coffee she had spilled on Saturday night's receipts. Her miserable walk in the rain. Padding around the house naked while Detective Davis snored the night away in her bedroom. Did he really want to hear *more?*

"Go back to the bubble bath," Cody murmured, surrounded by her fragrance, by the lyrical, dreamy sound of her voice. "You lost me there. You said something about putting peaches and cream into your—"

"Peaches and Cream bath crystals."

"Oh." He sounded vaguely disappointed. "Bathing in fresh fruit and cream sounded kind of exotic."

Suddenly, a fierce blast of wind hit the house, throwing the front door wide. Before Cody could rouse himself, Liza was up and across the room, closing the door against the driving rain. It took only seconds, yet the white cotton gown was sodden, clinging like gauze to her slight figure.

"I guess it's my day to play mermaid," she sighed, plucking at the sticky fabric. She glanced at Cody's shadow with a rueful smile just as the night exploded with sound and fury. Thunder rolled over the tiny cottage. Lightning tore a jagged edge from the night, spearing every corner of the room with blinding light. Liza felt herself flinch against the intrusion, her fingernails cutting welts into her palm. She found Cody's eyes through the assault, holding them. And holding them . . .

Cody felt his heartbeat rip into his throat. The image of Liza was burned into his heart and soul in one breathtaking moment. Her thin cotton gown was saturated, taking on the color and shape of the body beneath. He could see the perfect curves of her breasts, the darker shading of her nipples. Her lips were moist and parted, her eyelashes spiked with rain. Water glittered on her cheeks like tears.

Then light and sound perished. Liza trembled, blind in the sudden darkness. She wasn't sure what sense told her that Cody was crossing the room. Her arms were open to receive him, and then he was holding her, whispering her name again and again. Her slight body pressed against him, seeking and finding warmth. With the night exploding around them, they kissed, urgent, desperate kisses. Liza was shivering, twisting against him, trying to melt into his flesh so she would never have to let him go. She needed this moment to last forever.

Cody's hands were on her buttocks and he contin-ued to kiss her, pulling and lifting her hard against him. His tongue was fierce and probing, instinctively simulating the act of love. His hips ground against hers in the same primitive rhythm. More than he had ever wanted anything in his existence, he wanted her. He wanted to bury himself in her, he wanted to give and give. Her gown was twisted around her hips. His hands were pulling at his shirt, hot and fevered. Hungry. There was a wall behind her. Cody was lifting her, pressing her hard against the cold white adobe when the blood suddenly chilled in his veins.

Not like this.

His hands stilled on her breasts. The sound of his breathing was loud in the room. He found her eyes in the darkness, his own glittering with unresolved passion and numb shock. How strange that after all these years, the mere physical act would not be enough. Not with Liza. And how typical that he would choose this time and place to discover the heartrending difference between loving and making love.

No, not like this.

Moving her palms over his chest, Liza could feel the erotic tension. "What is it?" she whispered.

"I'm doing it all wrong," he said hoarsely.

She thought she might have heard him incorrectly. "What?"

His breath was harsh and his heart was thudding against his ribs, but he managed to whisper raggedly, "I want you. I want to take your soul out of your body and bring it together with mine. I want to give you things, the best things. But most of all, whatever else happens . . ."

"Yes?" The single word was barely a sigh.

"I want you to remember."

Her eyes filled with a slow, wondering light. Her head fell weakly back on her slender neck as he kissed the base of her throat with exquisite tenderness. Tenderness. What other man in the world would temper his passion for the sake of simple tenderness?

Cody lifted her in his arms, the damp gown tangled around her legs. He carried her effortlessly to the bedroom, placing her oh-so-gently on the tumbled bedcovers.

"Wait," he whispered. "I need to see you."

A moment later, the soft glow of the stone lamp on the dresser spilled into the room. Cody stood at the foot of the bed, his shirt hanging open over the uneven contractions of his rib cage. Lazy heat glittered in his heavy-lidded eyes. His smile reached out hesitantly, stroking her. There was such heaviness in the air. He wanted so much for her, to shower her with sensual gifts. The sensations kept flowing through him like a deep, hidden spring. Had this been any other woman, he would have been content and satisfied to merely let nature take its course. But this was Liza, and for Liza the world must be made perfect. He wanted to crowd this night with so much pleasure, so much joy, that the rest of her memories would fade into insignificance.

It might have been the first time for him. He moved slowly around the bed, dropping his clothes on the floor in a graceless heap. The muscles in his shoulders bunched with pure sexual tension, shimmering in the soft pool of light. His stomach was a

hard knot of desire. He knew so well what he wanted
to give her... if only he could conquer the mindless
demands of his own body.

Liza was curved on her side on the bed, one fist
pressed to her blood-hot cheek. Her pulse was trip-
ping in her throat, at her temples, deep within the
core of her femininity. She drew her knees up, pressing her thighs tightly together. The damp cotton
gown molded to her flesh, clinging, sensitizing the
heated skin. Her eyes were liquid gold, fixed on
Cody with a helpless intensity. Her breath caught in
her throat as he eased his weight gently on the side
of the bed, long legs stretched out next to hers. Side
to side, so close that she could see her own reflection
in his eyes, so close she could feel his breath stirring
the tendrils of hair at her temple. His hand moved in
thick slow motion, fingers trailing erotic, featherlight
patterns on her face, her neck, the flushed rise and
fall of her breasts.

Through a desert-dry throat, she whispered, "It
feels like a dream."

"No dream." He curved her slight body into his
arms, bringing her closer, acutely sensitive to the
light brush of her nipples over his chest. She saw his
pleasure, and she moved against him in a sweet, sensual massage. Her breasts strained against the semi-
transparent cotton, aching and full. She raised her
head blindly, trailing the tip of her tongue along the
hard curve of his jaw. Instinctively, her body
stretched out on the bed, straining closer, fitting into
the warm cradle of his hips.

The sensual heat in his eyes became a fire. His
hands closed over her shoulders, palms kneading in

rough, shaken circles. His mouth closed over hers, his tongue delicately urging her to openness. He altered the slant of his head, dragging her further in the kiss, so deep, so warm. Then his lips were on her throat, then lower still, closing over the turgid points of her breasts through the cotton fabric. The moisture of his mouth was exquisite torture, the hungry suckling motion arousing her to a quiet delirium.

"Let me." His voice was soft, husky. His hands were slipping beneath her gown, stroking the satin flesh of her bottom. She held on fiercely to his eyes, mesmerized by the pleasure and pain she saw in the sea-green depths. His hand slipped to her thigh, so tender, the intimate caress heating her blood. She caught her lower lip between her teeth as his fingers sought her warmth, tangling in silky curls, moving in a devastating, magical massage. Of their own accord, her hips began to move, pressing against the heel of his hand. Nerve chills rippled through her, and through him. Her muscles strained, and his hand deepened the pleasure. She pushed her fist against her mouth to stifle her cry.

"Don't," Cody whispered hoarsely. "It's only love. It's good, Liza . . . so good. Let yourself go. Just let it happen . . ."

Liza closed her eyes. She felt his fingers, strong, gentle, experienced, urging her higher. Shudders took her body. The warmth deep in the pit of her belly became an inferno, devouring conscious thought. Her muscles contracted harshly in hot, dizzying waves. And when she thought she could stand the tension no longer, his weight shifted on the mattress, and his mouth was making a hot, stroking circle where his fingers had been. She was mindless, shivering, fingers tangled fiercely in his hair. Then the unbearable tension spiraled in a whirlwind, exploding in a hot, devastating frenzy. For an endless moment, the present mingled with the future, and Liza's hold on it was tight. Then she drifted in a warm cocoon to earth, shimmering in radiance and honeyed heat.

"I've never... I didn't..." She couldn't find the words; she could barely find the oxygen to breathe. She saw Cody's face above her as if in a dream, disheveled hair limp with perspiration, a love flush staining his cheeks and smoldering in his eyes.

"It can be better," he said. "We can go so much higher together. We can go halfway to heaven and back, gypsy."

Liza was floating on a cloud of sunlight. Her eyes were wide and passion-drenched as he eased himself between her legs, catching her writhing hips in gentle hands. His own eyes were warm and blurred as he entered her, filling her with a deep, voluptuous heat. Liza was sated, yet she couldn't stop herself. Her spent muscles began to quiver, growing taut and hungry. Her body answered his demands, her breath coming in hard, racking shudders each time he thrust himself into her. She knew nothing beyond wet, intoxicating pleasure. She was woven into him, and could hardly distinguish his dampness from hers, her pleasure from his. She heard herself whisper his name as if from a distance, over and over. Desperate, primitive rhythms drew them together, soaring and dancing, touching and mating, spinning faster and faster until they escaped their fragile human control.

Blindly euphoric, trapped in streaming sunlight, they discovered sweet oblivion . . .

Later, spent but unwilling to surrender to sleep, they rested in quiet peace. The storm had weakened to a misty rain. Cody lay on his side next to Liza, one hand drifting slowly over her tousled curls. Liza turned her head sideways, her face nuzzling his palm. She was utterly, completely content.

When Cody finally spoke, his husky voice was little more than a whisper.

"You remember how fierce the storms can be in Colorado? How the sky can blow up around you with no warning and the thunder can echo from mountain to mountain?"

"I remember."

"One night two years ago, just after I was promoted to detective, I got a homicide call. It was a night like tonight, rain falling in sheets, lightning flashing over the mountains. And the thunder . . . I never heard thunder like that in my life, so loud you would have sworn it was coming from inside you. Anyway, I put on my old Dick Tracy raincoat with the collar pulled up, very official. I was a *detective*, man. I'd been around. I could deal with anything."

His eyes were bruised with the memories. Liza brushed his hair away from his forehead with awkward fingers. "Cody—"

"Shhh. I want you to hear this. There had been a gang fight on the East Side. I found a thirteen-year-old lying in a pool of his own blood, behind a dumpster. His skull had been cracked open with a baseball bat."

Liza had no words for him. She could only listen, hearing the dull, suspended agony in his voice.

"Between the sirens and the storm," he went on, "I didn't hear the kid on the fire escape above me. I just happened to look up. He was six stories high and shaking like a leaf. I don't know... maybe he thought the big, bad detective was going to shoot him." Cody paused, his hand finding Liza's. Softly, he continued, "He tried to jump from the fire escape to a window. He didn't make it."

"It wasn't your fault," Liza whispered.

"I know. It's just the memories that are hard to shake."

Liza curved against him, being very careful not to jar his injured shoulder. "I want your memories."

"What?"

"Your memories. All the bad ones, anything that hurts you. Give them to me."

His smile shaped against her hair. "Sweet gypsy. Why would I want to do that?"

"So I can throw them away. *Then*"—her voice was light, ingenuous—"I'll replace them with good memories. It may take me a while, but I can do it."

"Liza." He rolled on his back, his face suddenly young again, his smile a subtly tempting haze. "Sweet, sweet Liza... you already have."

Chapter

6

LIZA AND CODY slept through The Morning After. It was easy to miss, all things considered. The rain continued in a gray mist, heavy stormclouds diluted the sun, and the air was thick with a drowsy humidity. The cottage was dark and cool, one small lamp flickering weakly in Liza's bedroom. The tired light globe died with a little sigh just as Cody raised his groggy head.

"What time is it?" he murmured, gravel-voiced.

Liza's face was buried in her feather pillow. "Dunno. Don't care."

"I don't believe this. I'm *sore*, Liza."

With sleepy sympathy, she asked, "Your shoulder?"

"No, not my shoulder. My left ear."

"Oh." Liza turned over on her back and her shoulders began to quiver. "I'm sorry."

"You should be." Cody flopped back in the bed, his heavy-lidded eyes drifting closed. His hand found Liza's sleep-mussed hair, rubbing the cool strands between his fingers. Nice. Silky. He moved on to her face, fingers whispering over the tiny nose, the warm cheeks, the indescribable softness of her throat. And lower, becoming a featherlight caress on her breast.

Liza's gilt-edged lashes flickered open. "Cody?"

His hand was still busy, his eyes still closed. "Hmmm?"

"Your left ear . . . is it feeling any better?"

His eyes opened, and he gave her a smile of breathtaking sweetness. "You know . . . I believe it is."

That night Liza introduced Cody to the bubble bath.

"Grown men don't take bubble baths," Cody said, maintaining his macho image while he eased himself deeper and deeper in the steaming water. Musk-scented bubbles tickled the stubble on his chin.

Liza was sitting on the floor, elbows propped on the edge of the tub. She was dressed in Cody's wrinkled Hawaiian shirt and a smile. "Everyone takes bubble baths. They're the universal tranquilizer, far better than Valium. Besides, they're great for sore ears. What sort of music would you like?"

"You're going to sing?"

"Tape player. You have to set the scene for a perfect bubble bath. How do you feel about Ella Fitzgerald?"

"I'm ambivalent about Ella Fitzgerald," he said thoughtfully, shaping a bubble-goatee on his chin.

"But I'm stark, raving mad about Liza Carlisle. Can I ask you a question?"

Liza giggled, trailing her finger in the warm water. "You're sitting naked in my tub. You can ask me anything."

"Do you ever get homesick?"

Her manner was still playful, but something in her eyes told Cody he had hit a nerve. "I'm a big girl, Detective."

"You didn't answer the question, gypsy."

Still Liza hesitated, not because she didn't trust him, but because words were so inadequate and imprecise. It had taken her a lifetime to understand the only comfortable way of maintaining a relationship with her parents. How could she possibly make Cody understand in the space of a few sentences?

"Of course I miss my family," she said finally.

"How long has it been since you visited them?"

"Almost a year. I went home last Christmas." She paused, running her finger desultorily over his water-slick chest. "My parents tried for years and years before they finally had a child. I was their miracle baby. If I was happy, they were happy. If I was sad, they were sad. If I made a mistake, they were devastated. If I was ill, they were frantic. I was their *life*, Cody. Whatever I did, good or bad, had the most profound impact on them, completely out of proportion to a healthy parent-child relationship. I loved them, but having the entire responsibility for their emotions on my shoulders was turning that love into resentment. I moved away from home as much for their sakes as mine. I needed freedom. I needed to try my wings and be able to fall flat on my face once or twice without tearing them apart. They needed . . . an identity, for lack of a better word." She brightened, and the humor in her eyes tugged at his heart. "Do you remember when I told you my mother was president of the Junior League? She was never involved in anything like that before I left home. And my father took up golf, like a good doctor should, and they've traveled quite a bit . . . it's been good for all of us."

Cody took a deep breath, striving for lightness. "Tell me, gypsy . . . do you ever get tired of following the sun?"

The scent of his skin, musky and warm from the bath, surrounded her in a steamy, sensual cloud. It was suddenly difficult to concentrate. "Sometimes," she murmured, watching the steam collect in glittering droplets on his lashes. "Sometimes I want a brilliant vocation, my rightful place in the universe. But most of the time I want to see what's around the next corner more."

It wasn't the answer Cody would have liked. He shied away from the fear that whispered through him like a breath of cold air. He had time. There was still time to fit all the pieces of the puzzle in place. Anything was possible in this crazy world, even that mythical, magical prospect of living "happily ever after."

Anything, he told himself fiercely.

But for now, while the questions still remained, he refused to waste a single, precious moment. He was in love, a love that filled all the empty places in his soul.

And she was so close, her lips still faintly swollen . . .

Ten seconds later he was sharing his bath with a dripping, saucer-eyed gypsy in a flowered shirt. He kissed away her protests, promising to mop up the flood on the floor. And he rapidly developed a sincere appreciation for the bubble bath.

The morning after The Morning After, they stopped by Cody's hotel room for a change of clothes —his Hawaiian shirt had mysteriously shrunk—and rented a jeep for the drive to Copala.

"Wouldn't you like me to drive?" Liza asked, throwing a knapsack in the back of the jeep. "With your shoulder and everything?"

"My shoulder feels perfectly fine," Cody said. "Why the sudden urge to be the chauffeur?"

"I've never driven a stick-shift," she said wistfully, hooking her thumbs into the pockets of her jeans. "I've never been to Copala. I've never driven on a dirt track through a jungle. Think of all the new experiences I could have today."

"It boggles the mind." Cody pulled his baseball cap firmly on his head and slipped on a pair of sunglasses. "Get into the jeep, angel. No, no, no . . . the passenger's seat. Now buckle in."

Liza rolled her eyes in exasperation. "Cody—"

"Buckle in. I've never driven on a dirt track through the jungle, either. You might find yourself experiencing more than you bargained for today."

Two hours after leaving Mazatlán, they turned off the paved highway, bouncing merrily along a dusty road that looked as if it couldn't possibly lead anywhere. Liza was entranced regardless, throwing off her seat belt and taking pictures of the cameolike mountain scenery. The prospect of being lost didn't concern her in the least. Obviously, this was one of those blind corners she had talked about.

Cody was having a little difficulty getting into the spirit of the trip. Watching Liza's naive exuberance, her broad gestures, the smile that twisted her heart around her little finger, he felt like an observer in her very special game of life. He faced a little blind corner of his own, that of his contradictions. She was an exotic and whimsical creature, alive and intense and compelling. She possessed the identical "live for the moment" attitude that Cody Davis had turned into an art form. He admired her independence . . . and he feared it.

They came upon Copala in the early afternoon. Cody was triumphant, proclaiming his keen sense of direction, expert driving ability, and finely honed jungle survival skills. Liza was vaguely disappointed. She found it much more exciting when she wasn't sure of her destination. Still, the little town itself was a breathtaking moment out of time—a beautiful fortress church, quaint colonial houses, and narrow cobblestone streets, all nestled in an emerald-green paradise. They parked the jeep in the main plaza and toured the pueblo on foot, trailed by dozens of nine- and ten-year-old "guides." Liza chattered away in Spanish with her new young friends, translating to Cody with an amused expression.

"They want us to hire a burro and ride up to the mining area," she said. "They promise we will stumble upon valuable pre-Columbian artifacts to take home as souvenirs, not to mention rare and precious jewels. What do you think? I always wanted to go on a treasure hunt."

"Then I'm sure you will," Cody said lightly.

"Are you game? It won't take more than a couple of hours, at the most."

"It's going to be dark in a couple of hours," Cody replied.

Liza shrugged. "So we drive in the dark. It'll be fun."

Cody's nearest and dearest friends would have had little trouble recognizing the stubborn light in his eyes. "I'm not taking you over that miserable excuse for a road in the dark. I realize you love new experiences, and you've probably never spent the night stranded in the jungle, but you'll have to bear up under the disappointment. You're my responsibility, and I intend to get you back in one piece." *Ouch*. He sounded like a Girl Scout troop leader.

Liza was bewildered. Cody was more than just out of sorts today, he was...unpredictable. One moment he was happily reenacting *Romancing the Stone,* the next moment he was a tour guide with a schedule to keep. She watched him out of the corner of her eye, a subtle impression forming in her mind. He was just as confused with his quicksilver mood swings as she was.

Fortunately, by nature she was a peacekeeper. And she *would* keep peace with this exasperating hunk of contradictions, if it killed her. "Can I take a few minutes to visit the shops, O Prudent One? I saw some beautiful leather purses and silver jewelry."

"Shop away." Cody wasn't in the mood to bargain

with the local artists. He wanted to sit at a nice shady table near the plaza and brood. "I'm not really into leather purses. I'll grab a beer and wait for you by the jeep. Please remember we have to—"

Catching Cody off guard, she pulled his head down and kissed him hard on the mouth. Instinctively, with honeyed sweetness, they clung together, his hands twisted into her T-shirt at the sides of her body, her fingers twining themselves into his hair. His baseball cap bounced on the cobblestones.

"You needed that." Liza gave him a thick grin, the mischief dancing in her eyes. She picked up his hat and set it neatly on her own sun-drenched curls. "You are an extraordinarily sexy man, and I love to love you. Bye-bye."

After that, it was more of an effort to be depressed. Cody grabbed a warm beer—the only kind available—and drank it in the shade of a giant palm. He gave himself a nice little pep talk while he waited for his gypsy. This business of falling in love was new to him, but he wasn't doing too badly, all things considered. Yes, he was a little oversensitive where the lady was concerned. That probably came with the territory. He'd never been in this pitiful condition before, and he was't sure how to handle the side effects. Jealousy. Fear. Uncertainty. Possessiveness. The euphoric highs and the unexpected lows. All the little hobgoblins that played havoc with his basically cheerful disposition. He made a mental note to call Jenny long-distance and get some expert advice. If memory served him right, she had actually belted her husband during their tumultuous courtship. Today their blissful marriage was something out of a storybook, right down to the white picket fence that surrounded their townhouse. If Jenny Shapiro Coulter with the terrific right hook could navigate the rocky road of love, then Cody Davis could certainly do it.

He began to worry fifteen minutes later. There was no sign of Liza. The sun blazed down through the rarefied air, baking his skin through his clothes. He had another beer, and the worry curled up at the edges with anger. Where was she?

Eventually, he hit the outdoor market, trailing in and out of every single stall, fending off enthusiastic artists who greeted him with dollar signs in their eyes. He didn't speak Spanish, and his attempts to communicate met with blank-eyed stares. He managed to locate a silversmith who spoke broken English. Yes, the bright-haired young woman had stopped by his stall, looking at necklaces. One in particular she liked, but they could not agree on a price. If Cody would like to surprise her . . . ?

"I want to find her," Cody snapped, "not surprise her. Do you know where she went?"

The silversmith shrugged, scratching his head. "Away. I do not know. Her heart was broken, she wanted this necklace so badly. . ."

"Which necklace?" Cody sighed, wondering if all men fell in love with a whimper.

"This." An intricate silver chair was displayed, interlaced with lustrous turquoise stones. "For you, sir, and for the lovely miss, a special price today."

Cody left the shop with the necklace in his pocket and his temper on simmer. It had been over an hour since Liza had wandered off. This was Mexico, for

Pete's sake. Anything could have happened to her.

He jogged back to the plaza, pacing the length of the jeep. The sky was taking on a tired reddish tinge. Another thirty minutes and he would contact the local authorities. Provided there was such a thing in Copala . . .

While he was glaring south, into the sunset, Liza snuck up behind him, tapping him lightly on the shoulder. Cody whirled, a muscle working fiercely in his cheek.

"Hi," Liza said softly, her golden eyes wary. The pocket of her shirt was torn. Her face was striped with dirt. Her hair had become home to a miniature collection of flora and fauna, topped with his dusty baseball cap.

Cody was relieved, angry, curious, frustrated. Somewhere far in the back of his mind, a little voice told him the sane thing to do. *Take her in your arms, hold her, ask if she's hurt. Find out what happened as calmly and tenderly as you can.*

But a man in love was seldom sane.

In a voice that he wasn't able to keep under complete control, he said, "Let me guess. You hopped on the old burro and went for a treasure hunt."

"No. Not exactly." Liza busied herself brushing the dust off her jeans. Something small and brown dropped out of her hair and crawled away on the street. She knocked off the baseball cap with a muffled yelp and shook out her hair with a vengeance.

"Then where," Cody asked softly, dangerously, "where the bloody, hopping *hell* have you been the past three hours?"

"I wasn't gone three hours." She threw back her

hair, flushed and breathless. "I was gone one hour and twenty minutes. I have a watch."

"I have a watch, too." There wasn't a breath of humor in the smile he gave her. "I've been looking at it every two minutes. Answer my question."

"I went shopping." Liza took off her sneakers and tossed them into the jeep. Cody noticed for the first time that they were caked in mud. "I bought a purse. Damn. I left it in the mine. I'll never find it again."

Cody held her gaze for a long, silent moment. She began to hop on the sun-baked cobblestones. He lifted her in his arms, depositing her none too gently in the jeep. He picked up his cap, dusted it off, slammed it on his head, and got behind the wheel.

"What mine?" he said.

Liza sighed, glancing sideways through her lashes. The setting sun washed his skin with a rainbow of color, adding to the fire in his eyes. "You're not going to like it."

"What mine?"

"The one I got lost in." She held up a hand when he opened his mouth. "No, let me finish. It's no big deal, I promise. I went shopping. I looked at some jewelry, I bought a purse. I was on my way back here when I noticed an empty mine shaft on the hill above the church. It wasn't far, maybe a hundred yards. I didn't want to come all the way to Copala and not even look for just a *little* treasure."

Cody nodded his head, drumming his fingers on the steering wheel. "I should have known."

"I was only going to take a quick look. The problem was, inside the mine there were all these tunnels going every which way, and I got turned around. It

took me a while to find my way back out. Anyway,
here I am, safe and sound. I'm sorry I kept you waiting. It was a dumb trick."

Cody started the jeep without a word. He drove
to Daniel's, a small restaurant at the entrance to Copala. He vaulted over the side of the jeep, talked
briefly with a woman shelling corn on the shaded
porch, and got back behind the wheel.

"It's up to you," he said. "We can try to make the
drive to Mazatlán in the dark. We could have all
kinds of fun adventures. Roll the jeep, drive off a
cliff, freeze our buns off in this nice mountain air. It's
almost irresistible, isn't it? Or we can be dull and
conservative and drive to Villa Blanca for the night."

Liza was treading carefully. "Villa Blanca? What's
that?"

"A small pueblo just south of here. I was just told
they have a hotel and restaurant. Hey, I don't know
about you, but I'm all for risking life and limb."

Liza was developing a nasty headache. "I said I
was sorry, Cody."

What the hell was he doing? Without thinking,
without daring to think, Cody jammed the jeep into
gear, turning south on the rutted track. Liza didn't
have to be told to buckle her seat belt. Cody was
driving with smooth, capable recklessness . . . if there
was such a thing. He picked his targets carefully,
going only for the dips, branches, and boulders that
would jar the jeep without actually damaging it. He
lost his hat. Liza's shoes bounced on the floor like
chocolate-covered jumping beans.

Ten minutes into the harrowing ride, Cody
slammed on the brakes, bringing the jeep to a halt in

a choking cloud of dust. His profile was blurred in a crimson sunset, and it was difficult to see his expression. Liza held her breath.

"I need a sign," Cody said, staring straight ahead.

"What?" Liza glanced around uncertainly, wondering if they had missed a turnoff for Villa Blanca. It didn't seem likely, as the dirt road had been walled by solid jungle since leaving Copala.

"I need a sign," he repeated, tilting his head back against the seat. "I need to wear it around my neck. It should say, 'Be patient with me, I'm temporarily lost.'"

Liza swatted at a mosquito. She didn't know which was worse, being a sitting target for the vampires of the jungle, or having her fillings jarred loose with Cody's ferocious driving. "Cody, I think your fever might be back."

"I'm serious." He met her eyes, and his voice became suddenly tight and soft. "I'm lost, I'm clumsy, I'm reckless. Now I know why they call it *falling* in love. It isn't something you can do with a hell of a lot of grace."

Love. The word trickled with a cold shock through Liza's mind. For the last few days, her subconscious had been busy dodging that particular word. Love meant complications. As long as she didn't face the fact that she was falling in love with Cody, those complications would never materialize. Thus spoke the hopeful, if slightly blind, optimist.

Unsteady pulses danced in strange places inside her. "You didn't love me an hour ago."

"I did." His arm stretched across the back of the

seat, fingers tracing the ultrasensitive folds of her ear. "I did."

"You have a strange way of showing it."

"I realize that." Cody sighed, his expression more open than she had ever seen it before. "I'm hoping to get better at this with a little practice. Right now I'm wandering around blind. I'm reacting with my heart instead of my head for the first time in my life." His smile was faintly rueful, and very, very human. "I don't know what I'm going to do next."

"I do," Liza whispered.

She leaned across the seat, meeting him halfway. His lips closed over hers, touching her with gentle, unhurried eroticism, then drew away. He gave her a smile that made her forget her doubts and misgivings. She nearly forgot to breathe.

"So," he said softly, "have you got anything to say, gypsy?"

"You drive too fast."

"Yeah."

"You're accident prone."

"You'll get used to it."

She dragged him back into the kiss, with as much enthusiasm as her seat belt would allow. "I need a sign, too," she said.

Chapter

7

LIZA COULDN'T SLEEP. There was no rhyme or reason to her insomnia. The bed at Villa Blanca had an honest-to-goodness feather mattress and was sinfully comfortable. The room was charming in an Old World style, with white stucco walls and a terra-cotta floor. The view of the mountains from the tiny balcony was magnificent.

The company wasn't bad, either.

Liza sat cross-legged at the foot of the bed, staring at her sleeping roommate with cheerful intensity. She had once read that a person's true character was revealed when he slept. What, then, could she discover about Cody? He rested peacefully, which indicated either a clear conscience or a thoroughly exhausted individual. Her memory drifted back over the past two hours, the color building in her cheeks. Possibly a thoroughly exhausted individual with a

clear conscience. A tiny, forgotten smile drifted over
his lips. Obviously a satisfied individual. A light tang
of perspiration oiled his body. A hard-working individual.

After several minutes of this, the warmth in her
face spread to other parts of her body. She slipped on
Cody's shirt—wearing his clothes was becoming a
habit—and quietly opened the sliding door to the
balcony. A brisk dip in the cool mountain air should
be just as effective as a cold shower.

He found her there twenty minutes later. She was
sitting on the edge of the low stucco wall, bare legs
dangling deliciously over the side. She had braided
her hair earlier to help keep it tangle-free, and a fat
coil hung halfway down her back, tied with one of
Cody's fluorescent shoelaces. One made do in these
situations.

"You're going to fall," he said.

At the sound of his voice she started, and nearly
did. "Don't sneak up on me like that. I could have
gone head over heels into the bougainvillaea."

He'd pulled on his jeans, though he hadn't both-
ered to snap them up. His hair was ruffled around his
face, softening the lean planes and angles. His eyes
were soft with sleep. "I had this horrible dream," he
said huskily. "I was sleeping in this little hotel room
in Villa Blanca with the most beautiful woman in the
world in my arms. Then I woke up, and I was all
alone." He paused, then added sadly, "My shirt was
gone, too."

Liza grinned over her shoulder, wide awake and
appreciating the view. "It must have been horrible."

"I don't think I'll ever get over it." He moved behind her, his arms closing around her waist, his chin resting on her shoulder. The crisp night air caught her fragrance, swirling it around him like a siren's song. Beyond the moonlit hillside, the night took on a savage darkness. "So why are you sitting on the balcony at two in the morning?"

"I couldn't sleep."

"Why didn't you wake me?"

Liza snuggled back against him, savoring his delicious male warmth. "You earned your rest. Besides, I was enjoying myself. This night feels like a fairy tale."

He pressed his lips to the nape of her neck. "This night feels cold."

"You have no romance in your soul. Look out there. The darkness could swallow you forever. And listen . . . when the trees move, they're whispering secrets. It's a night for wizards and unicorns and witches . . . all the good stuff."

"And here you wait on your balcony, like Rapunzel's shameless sister."

One side of her mouth curved up. "Depraved, aren't I?"

"Speaking of which . . ." He pulled her neatly off the balcony, twirling her in his arms with a move Fred Astaire would have envied. "Come inside with me. I don't like you out of my sight."

Moonlight accented the childish solemnity of her expression. "Then we may have a problem. Gypsies are always disappearing, you know. We can't help it. It's part of our nature."

"That's nothing a good strong piece of rope can't cure."

"You can't *restrain* us. That's barbaric."

"My darling gypsy, I'd lock you up in your steamer trunk if I thought I could get away with it. Are you coming inside?"

"Do I have a choice?"

"Of course you do." He smiled, that damned adorable, charming, sweetly innocent smile. "Walk or be carried."

Cody woke just before dawn, roused by a vaguely troubling dream. He reached out in the darkness, finding Liza by his side. He curved to her warmth, and was able to doze off again. How he loved having her near.

On the drive back to Mazatlán, Cody indulged Liza's passion for new experiences. He strapped himself firmly in the passenger's seat and put the jeep at her mercy. After a slow start—several of them, as a matter of fact—Liza caught on to the mysteries of the clutch and the gearshift. Cody watched her navigate the narrow mountain roads, her hair whipping in a wild curtain around her shoulders, her lower lip caught between her teeth. He knew without a shadow of a doubt that she was the best thing that had ever happened to him.

He was still determined to give them both time, but the longer he knew Liza, the more certain he was that he wanted to commit himself to her. He hadn't talked to her about commitment. He didn't really know what that word would mean to her. There was still so much he had to learn about Liza. He only knew that she was an enchanting and delightful addiction, and he would never weary of being with her. She had come into his small universe like light through a prism, making him see and hear and feel things he never thought possible. She was uniquely and completely herself, never afraid to be unusual or unconventional. She touched him in his heart, and he wanted nothing more than to hold her in his sight forever.

The following days flowed one into another, a sparkling, sunny, radiant haze of Liza-watching. Memories to cherish... Liza sitting on the floor in his hotel room, learning to play poker... Liza dancing gleefully on the deck of a chartered fishing boat, cheering the huge marlin that had escaped his line ... Liza flopping out of the surf in snorkel, fins, and a white bikini...

And tonight. Liza beneath the dusty white spotlight at the cantina, smiling at him, at him alone. She was singing a Spanish ballad in her rich, smoky voice. Cody didn't understand a word she was saying, but her message was achingly clear. He wondered what good old Juan would do if he picked her up and carried her out the door.

"She's something, isn't she?" A florid-faced tourist with tequila breath slipped in next to Cody at the bar. "Nice pair of lungs on that one."

Cody found a table adjacent to the stage. Nearby he heard a party of college kids offer the waiter fifty bucks for Liza's phone number. Cody could have told them she didn't have a phone, if his teeth weren't clenched together quite so tightly.

Cody moved to the shadows in the back of the room. Good old Juan sent a drink on the house, with a little note: *Our Liza is breaking hearts tonight.*

Our Liza. Cody brooded on that while Liza took requests from the happy crowd of tourists. One glassy-eyed gentleman requested her address. Another party animal wanted to hear "Baby It's You," and complimented Liza on her dress.

Cody took a good hard look at her dress. It was soft and white, with a full, embroidered ruffle that could be worn on or off the shoulders. She wore it off the shoulders, revealing tantalizing glimpses of rounded flesh. Cody would have preferred it on the shoulders, if she had asked him. Which she hadn't.

When the set ended, Cody couldn't get her off the stage fast enough. He was tired of sharing her with so many eyes. He wanted her to himself. He told her she was cold and put his jacket over her shoulders. Liza laughed and told him not to be silly and gave the jacket right back. Cody said he wanted an early night and pulled her through the jostling crowd.

Juan intercepted them in the vestibule. He was wearing a beige linen suit and a cool air of sophistication. His smile was a dazzling flash of light in his sun-browned face. "Liza, I'm glad I caught you. Where are you going in such a rush?"

"What a good question," Liza murmured, arching her brow in Cody's direction. "Where are we going in such a rush, Detective?"

"It's a surprise," Cody said. "We all know how you love surprises, Liza."

"Then she should love what I have to say to her." Juan slipped his arm around Liza's shoulders, hugging her lightly. "*Querida*, we leave on Monday."

"Do we?" Liza asked cheerfully. "And where are we going?"

"I have some business with a friend of mine who lives in Cancun. He is sending his private plane for me first thing Monday morning. Time and again you've told me how you would enjoy visiting the Mayan ruins. There is no reason in the world why you should not fly down with me and play tourist while I complete my business."

Cody's expression said quite clearly that he could think of one or two reasons. Evidently sensitive to the hostile vibrations coming from that direction, Juan added smoothly, "And of course the invitation includes your friend the detective. Mr. Davis, I hope you can join us?"

"Cody, a trip to Cancun!" Liza was already anticipating, brown eyes wide and shining. "Better yet, a *free* trip to Cancun. I've wanted to go there *forever*."

"Sounds great." Cody wasn't thinking. Subconsciously, he had made a decision. He had just spent a long evening watching men watching Liza. At the moment, he was buddy-buddy with the old green-eyed monster, jealousy. If someone would have asked him just what it was he was jealous *of*, he probably couldn't have answered. He only knew that he wanted reassurance. "It really sounds great. I'm sorry I can't make the trip."

Liza's smile went out like a light. "Why not?"

"I only have a few more days left in Mexico, Liza. I haven't really seen much of Mazatlán yet. You go ahead. If you've wanted to see Cancun forever, you shouldn't pass up this opportunity."

Liza was still for a moment. Then she turned to Juan, her eyes brilliant, the curve of her lips cool and detached. "I'm sorry, Juan. We can't make it. But I do appreciate the offer."

Juan shrugged, glossing over the tension that shivered in the air. "Another time, perhaps."

"I hope so." She looked steadily at Cody. "Are you ready to leave?"

Outside, he asked her if she wanted to take a cab. She didn't answer, but kept right on walking. She was afraid to examine the fears that curdled in the pit of her stomach. She took refuge in her anger.

"Are you happy?" she asked suddenly, stopping dead in the middle of the sidewalk.

It was a bad question. Cody wasn't entirely sure what he was at the moment, but "happy" didn't ring a bell. "Shouldn't I be?"

Liza shrugged. "I just wondered. You ought to be happy. You got exactly what you wanted, didn't you? You pulled the strings, and I danced."

There was a pause. "Are you talking about the trip to Cancun?"

"You know damn well I am." The breeze caught her hair, lifting it up and away from her face. "You wanted to manipulate me back there, and you did. I don't know why. You gave me an ultimatum. I could go to Cancun—alone—or stay with you. You *wanted* me to have to choose."

"It wasn't like that."

"Cody, I've had enough experience with emotional blackmail to recognize it when I see it." She smiled, but only with her mouth. Her eyes were shuttered. "I never expected it from you. Maybe I don't like surprises as much as I thought."

"All right. We need"—he raised a hand and flagged down a *pulmonia*—"to talk."

"I don't want to talk."

That he expected. He took hold of her arm, giving her a little gentle assistance into the *pulmonia*. "You don't need to talk. You just need to listen."

The ride to the Camino Real was silent. The walk through the lobby was silent, as was the elevator ride. She was certainly doing *her* part, Liza thought, listening to him breathe.

Cody unlocked the door to his room, then stepped aside to let her enter. Liza walked into a fairy tale. The room was bathed in the flickering glow of candlelight. A cold supper was arranged on the table near the window, a bottle of champagne chilling in an ice bucket. A small gift-wrapped package rested on a silver-rimmed plate.

"What's this?" she said softly.

"*This* is actually a little inconvenient at the moment," Cody muttered, flickering a wry glance at the long-stemmed roses in a crystal vase beside the bed. "We had to come back here, though. I was afraid if we didn't, the candles might burn the place down. I bribed a room-service waiter to light them at exactly eleven o'clock."

A silver branch of candles stood on the dresser, casting a restless golden shadow on the wall. Liza walked over to them, skimming her finger lightly through the flames. "What are you celebrating?"

"You," he said. "Don't do that, you'll burn yourself."

She met his eyes. "Not if you do it fast enough.

Then you just feel the warmth. You're gone before the flame can burn you."

He crossed the room to the window, staring out at the dark void that was the ocean. "There's a wealth of Freudian meaning in that statement," he said quietly, "but I don't think I want it explained to me."

She went to him, circling his waist with her bare arms, pressing her face into the hollow of his spine. "You can't push me, Cody. I won't be pushed."

"I know that." His hands closed over hers at his waist, fingers rubbing gently across her knuckles. "I don't know what drives me lately. The last thing in the world I want to do is hurt you."

"Back at the cantina . . . why didn't you want to go to Cancun with me?"

"It's complicated." Cody saw his own grim smile reflected in the window, Liza's huge eyes over his shoulder. "I'm not even sure that I understand. You and I . . . we're so careful not to talk about the future. We just live from minute to minute, and leave all the questions unasked and unanswered. Tonight I saw a chance to have one of those questions answered."

"Mazatlán with you or Cancun with Juan? A little test?"

"Something like that."

Candlelight bathed the room in quiet shadows. Liza's hands dropped to her sides, feeling heavy and useless. "Don't do that to me," she said helplessly. "Don't do that to *us*."

Cody faced her. With infinite gentleness, he stroked the hair from her flushed cheek. His smile was faint and flickering, like the candlelight. "Remember when I said I needed a little time to find my way with you?"

Liza turned her face, pressing her lips to his palm. "Yes."

"I think I need a little more time. I'm developing a healthy respect for anyone who's fallen in love without going quietly out of their mind."

"You're doing just fine . . . considering."

"Considering what?"

She lifted her head, kissing the firelight from his lips. So warm. "Considering you're such a *conservative* kind of guy. All this raw emotion and unbridled passion can't be easy for you."

"I'll show you unbridled passion," Cody muttered, backing her inexorably toward the bed with slow, deliberate steps. "I'll show you conservative. I'll show you raw emotion."

She stopped him with a hand over his mouth. "First . . ."

"Hmmm?"

"First show me what's in the box." Her cheeks were soft with childish enthusiasm, her eyes warm as melting toffee. "You know how I am about surprises. They make me crazy. I wonder and I wonder—"

He stopped her with a hand over her mouth. "You're so cute when you beg. Sit down on the sofa."

Liza sat. The sofa was actually a rattan love seat with serviceable earth-tone cushions.

"I picked it up in Copala while you were treasure-hunting." Cody settled himself on the carpet at her feet, one long leg drawn up as an armrest. He arranged the satin bow on the box with heart-tugging attention to detail, then put it gently in Liza's lap.

"It's not much," he said. "Just a token of my affliction."

"I'm sure you meant affection," Liza murmured, the corners of her mouth stretching into charming dimples.

"I'm sure I did. Open it." Cody watched the expressions chasing one another across her face with pure enjoyment. Curiosity. Anticipation. Surprise, with a heavy dose of round brown eyes. And such delight . . . his first impulse was to rush right out and buy her something else, so he could watch the process all over again.

"This necklace," she whispered, holding the rich silver up to the candlelight. "How did you know? I saw this when I was shopping in Copala . . ."

"And I saw it when I was hunting for you in Copala. The silversmith told me you had admired it. Liza?"

"What?"

"Don't do that, honey."

The beautiful necklace was blurred with her tears. "Don't do what?"

"Don't cry. We Charles Bronson types can't deal with a weeping woman. It unmans us."

"I'm not crying, Charlie. My eyes are glistening. Will you help me put it on?"

He went up on his knees, fastening the clasp at the back of her neck while she held her hair to the side. Cody's fingers were too big for the delicate chain, and it took him a minute or two. "I've almost got it . . . there." He sat back on his heels, admiring the flash of silver and turquoise that rose and fell on her lovely chest. The necklace became her. Hell, a strand of paper clips would become her. "I do love you, you know," he said almost absently.

Liza met his eyes, fingering the cool silver at her throat. She hadn't said the words yet, not out loud. She was a product of Jeremy's cold-blooded tutoring. Letting down her guard was something that came in bits and pieces, with effort. Yet something about tonight felt different. Her smile came slowly, and her hair tickled the side of his face as she leaned down to him. "You know something?" she whispered. "I'm beginning to think that I was never in love before."

"Before what?" Cody's voice sounded thick and strange.

"Before you."

She caught him off guard, tumbling on the floor, showering an avalanche of kisses on his face. Rolling, they clung together with reckless, glutted sweetness until a collision with the bed table brought them up short.

"Hey, Detective." Liza was on top, holding him prisoner in a tumbling cascade of hair. "Want to show me where you keep your gun?"

Chapter

8

"WHAT AM I EATING?" Cody asked.

"Tamales, frijoles, toasted chili peppers." Liza pointed to a clay dish in the center of the table. "And *that* is turkey."

It wasn't a cozy dinner for two. Mazatlán was celebrating a fiesta. The plaza across from the yellow-towered cathedral was strung with paper lanterns, balloons, and streamers. There was continuous street dancing, with a band every hundred yards. Now and then a burst of fireworks would light up the sky, raining ashes into the harbor. The voices of the boisterous revelers rose in song, making conversation difficult for those seated at the sidewalk cantinas. Liza and Cody's table was an attempt by an ingenious proprietor to take advantage of the swelling crowds. It wasn't actually *on* the sidewalk, but in the street, wedged tightly between a popcorn vendor and a watercolor exhibit.

"It doesn't look like turkey," Cody said.

"What?"

He shouted. "It doesn't look like turkey. It looks like chocolate pudding with lumps."

"Close. It's shredded turkey cooked in a sauce made of chocolate, spices, and sesame seeds." Liza giggled, pointing her fork at him. "Your face is as red as a chili pepper. Are you sure this food agrees with you?"

"It's a little hot," Cody said, "but I'm enjoying it."

"As much as you enjoyed our candlelight dinner in your hotel room last night?"

Cody fixed her with sleepy green eyes. "We never ate last night."

"Oh." Liza smiled at the sky. "We didn't, did we?"

Cody forked a piece of the turkey in his mouth and barely tasted it. He was blissfully absorbed in the woman opposite him. Liza shone like a jewel in this setting. Colored lights from the paper lanterns threw her face into soft, hazy shadows. Her hair fell in rippling waves to her shoulders, lifting and swirling with the slightest breath of air. She wore a white silk blouse with a deep, gathered neckline and a bright blue skirt tied with a yellow sash. The necklace Cody had given her sparkled silver fire at her throat.

And she was too far away.

Cody pushed his plate aside, reaching in his back pocket for his wallet. "What do you say we settle the bill and find a nice, crowded street to dance in? I have an uncontrollable urge to hold you."

"You should never fight uncontrollable urges," she said wisely. "It isn't healthy."

"Definitely *not* a lesson learned at Mommy's knee." While Cody was hunting for money in his wallet, his airline ticket slipped out and fluttered to the ground. Liza quickly picked it up, brushing the flecks of popcorn off the white vellum paper.

"What do we have here?" she murmured. "You know, I think a man's wallet is far more interesting than —*oh*." After a tense pause: "This is your airline ticket."

"Right in one." Cody took it from her and placed it back in his wallet, but not before he had seen the date printed on the front. November thirteenth. Two days away. It was something he had constantly pushed to the back of his mind, the time limit on paradise. Forty-eight hours. "Would you like to dance now?"

Liza's smile was as hollow as her voice. "Of course. I'd love to."

They pushed their way into the tiled plaza, jostled by merrymakers in long, bearded masks and tourists in madras shorts. The fireworks cast twitching, flame-bright patterns on the shifting crowd. The band was playing the melancholy "La Paloma." Liza went into Cody's arms like a stick puppet. She felt empty inside, as if he had already gone. She knew he was waiting for her to talk about the future. She also knew he couldn't wait forever. If only she weren't so afraid . . .

"You're shivering," Cody said after a few minutes of awkward dancing. "Would you like a drink to warm you up? I know I could use one." He pulled her through the crowd to a vending cart topped with a striped parasol. "What have we here?"

"*Pulque*," Liza said. "It's an alcoholic drink made from maguey plants. It's very strong, I don't know if—"

"I knew these people were getting their rosy cheeks from somewhere. *Dos, señor!* I need a little inspiration tonight."

It wasn't the only time Cody visited the *pulque* cart. He became fast friends with the proprietor. He tried orange and raspberry flavors. His dancing improved. His mood took a turn for the worse.

"Smile, Liza." He had a drink in his hand, holding it high above the dancing crowd. His hair was wind-ruffled and wild, high spots of color burning his cheeks. "If I didn't know better, I'd think you weren't having a good time."

"Whatever gave you that idea?" Her voice was steady. For some reason she remembered what Jeremy had been like in one of his "moods," all reckless fury. Her job had been to calm him down. Calm him and soothe him and reassure him. She'd learned to keep a steady voice at all costs.

"You aren't smiling. Maybe you're tired." Cody spotted an empty table at the edge of the plaza. "We'll sit for a while and watch the fireworks."

Halfway to the table, Miller O'Keefe materialized before them like a blond genie. He was wearing white slacks and a red shirt with two horizontal stripes across the chest. His glorious hair was pulled straight back and tied at the back of his neck with a leather strap. He looked like a pirate with a funky sense of fashion. "Good wine needs no bush," he announced cheerfully, planting an enthusiastic kiss on Liza's cheek. "Davis, it's good to see you. And now that the niceties are over, can I borrow your woman? I want to dance with her."

Liza had her mouth open to refuse when Cody said quite clearly, "She's not my woman, Miller. Liza's very much her own person. She does *only* what she wants to do. It's kind of a religion with her."

Miller whistled soundlessly, then turned to Liza with bright blue eyes. "Well. One of us just got told off. I've had too much tequila to be sure just who."

"I'd like to dance, Miller." Liza barely glanced at Cody. She was hurting inside, how she was hurting. The road she was traveling with Cody was looking more and more familiar. Once upon a time, Jeremy had talked to her with just that tone in his voice, part accusation, part bitter hostility. "I'll be back in a few minutes, Cody."

One dance turned into two. The musicians played a *jarabe*, the dance of gypsies and peasants. The rhythm began to seep into Liza's body, loosening her muscles, bringing her a needed distraction. She danced until the blood was hot in her temples, and her hair was a tangled cloud. Bathed in the reflected glow from the lanterns, she raised her skirt to her ankles, then her knees, then let it drop. She danced faster, her shoulders shimmering with perspiration. The tension she felt melted away, replaced by a soothing optimism. Somehow everything would work out. Somehow.

Cody was waiting at the table when Miller brought her back. "That was quite an exhibition," he said lightly. He stood up with a lazy grace, all emotion concealed behind his opaque eyes. He was again hiding behind that professional mask he wore so well. "Liza, you didn't tell me you could dance like a gypsy. Sit down, Miller. I'll buy you a drink."

"No, thank you." There was absolutely no regret in Miller's voice. "I could tell the two of you were having a very... special... evening when I intruded. You just go back to doing whatever it was you were doing. Maybe later on in the evening we'll have another dance."

Cody stared at Miller's retreating back. "Did Miller mention how long he was staying in Mazatlán?"

"No, he didn't. He doesn't seem like the type to make definite plans."

"Then he'll probably be around for a while yet." Cody picked up his glass, saw that it was empty and put it down again. "Would you like to dance?"

"No, thank you." So polite, like a schoolgirl.

"Another drink?"

"I've had enough to drink," she said, studying her clasped hands on the table. "We both have."

Cody raised his eyebrows, an odd smile curving his lips. "You're probably right. If I had another drink, I'd probably say something I'd regret... like asking you why the hell you danced like that with Miller."

Liza took a deep, painful breath. "Cody—"

"Wouldn't it have been easier just to hand him your house key? Oh, I forgot. You don't have one. Your door is wide open day and night, isn't it, gypsy?"

She waited until she knew her knees would sup-

port her. Then she stood, very slowly. She looked at
the empty glass on the table, then at Cody. "Why
don't you go ahead and have another one?" she suggested sweetly. "Alcohol brings out the real you,
Cody."

The crowd swallowed her in an instant. Liza con-
centrated fiercely on putting one foot in front of the
other, as if it were the most difficult task she would
ever have to do.

Cody's bags were packed. Shirts and slacks had
been dropped in the old suitcase one on the other,
socks stuffed in the corners. He'd called the airlines
and moved his flight ahead a day.

He had a perfect view of the fireworks display
from his hotel room window. They seemed to go on
forever. Shirtless, he walked out on the balcony,
smelling the sulphur in the wind. A tiny cinder fell
on his shoulder, burning. A baby scar was born.

So much emptiness . . .

It was there in the air around him, the quiet desperation. He didn't know how to deal with it. He
couldn't go to her. Despite his best intentions, he
continued to hurt her. He was anxious to be gone
now, to give her the peace of his absence.

He was taking home a brand-new perspective of
himself. Cody Davis was finally capable of fear. He
was afraid of the future. How would he readjust to
life without Liza?

A soft knock sounded at the door. The maid to
turn down his bed, Cody thought, walking back in
the room. She did it every night, placing two mints
on the pillows. Liza had discovered one smashed on

the sheets just this morning. The memory brought the ghost of a smile to his lips.

He opened the door, prepared to banish the helpful maid and her chocolate mints. Instead, he found Liza.

It took him a moment to be sure she was really there, and not a product of his alcohol-befuddled mind. But then he registered that it was indeed Liza, still in the clothes she had worn at the carnival, her eyes shimmering like a doe's, soft and intense.

"Can I come in?" she said, filling the brittle, startled silence.

"Of course. I'm sorry." Cody stood aside to let her pass. He closed his eyes briefly, his shoulders taut with strain. Frustration burned the muscles in his throat.

She walked into the room, pausing by the open suitcase on his bed. She touched a shirt, rubbing the soft cotton between her thumb and forefinger. "You're packing?"

"Yes."

"You're leaving early." It was a statement, not a question.

"Yes."

"I went walking," she said. She hadn't looked at him since she came into the room; she didn't look at him now. "I needed some time. I wanted to be absolutely sure that I didn't do anything I'd regret." She drew back her hand and slapped him hard, *hard* across the face. Cody could have stopped her in the blink of an eye. Liza knew it; she also knew he wouldn't. "You're a selfish bastard," she said, breathing hard. "I'd never be able to give you enough, would I, Cody? I finally figured that out tonight. I could love you with all my heart, but you'd want more. You'd want to *own* me. You're no different than Jeremy. Oh, you've got more subtlety, maybe, more of that boyish charm that makes it go down a little easier. You're still two sides of the same coin."

Cody's gaze remained steadily on her, his lips drawn. "Who's Jeremy?"

Her eyes burned him. "Look in the mirror."

"Sit down, Liza," he said softly.

"I don't think so. I've said everything I wanted to say. Have a nice flight, Detective."

"I *said*"—his hands curved over her shoulders and he pushed her down on the edge of the bed—"sit the bloody hell down."

Liza's fingers closed around the bedspread in a death grip. She told him with her eyes that he had won a temporary victory only. He was bigger than she was, not to mention his black belt in karate. If he wanted her to sit, more than likely she would end up sitting. "Yes, master," she said with barbed sweetness. "I have sat the bloody hell down. What comes next?"

"You're going to tell me about Jeremy."

"Am I?" She considered this for a moment, then shrugged. "All right. It won't change anything. Jeremy was my friend when I was going to college in New York. Then he was my lover . . . then he was my sovereign lord and king. At least, he thought he was."

Cody let his gaze study every line and curve of her face. "What happened?"

Liza looked around the room, as if searching for a

friendly face. Her eyes were cloudy; she was remembering. "He began to resent anything I did that took me away from him. Anything or anyone. He screened my calls, alienated my friends, monopolized every moment of my time. His jealousy destroyed everything we had together. It nearly destroyed me."

Cody was silent, listening to the heady sound of his own heartbeat. After a moment, he said, "I don't want to own you, Liza."

"No?" Her reflected gaze lifted to his. "What would you call it, then?"

"Love."

"Love." She repeated the word as if it were worthy of closer inspection. "People in love don't hurt each other, Cody. They don't test each other. They don't try to control each other."

"If you really believe that, you don't know as much about love as you thought, Liza." He was staring blindly at the wall above her head, every muscle in his body taut and stinging. "You can hurt someone you love as easily as anyone else."

She didn't say anything. What was there left to say? She stood up, fighting the most terrifying sense of loss. The pull on the mattress sent a shirt tumbling off the pile of chaos in Cody's suitcase. She picked it up automatically, then her gaze was caught by a photograph tucked into Cody's belongings. The shirt dropped from her nerveless fingers.

Too late, Cody realized what she had seen. "Liza—"

"Why do you have my photograph?" She was distantly surprised to hear the even tenor of her voice.

"That picture was taken last year at Christmas. Who gave it to you?"

"Your father," Cody said quietly.

Liza looked from Cody to the photograph and back again. Two spots of color burned high in her cheeks. "I don't understand. You know my father?"

"Yes." Cody raised his hand to touch her, but she flinched away. Her eyes were cold.

"How?" she whispered. "When did you meet him?"

"Two years ago, he took a bullet out of my shoulder. Last month he stitched me up after the robbery attempt." There was absolutely no expression in Cody's voice. He might have been reciting the alphabet.

"He's your physician? Why didn't you tell me?" She picked up the photograph carefully, as if it might burn her. "Why did he give you my picture?"

"He asked me to check up on you."

"Let me get this straight." Liza took a deep breath, but no oxygen seemed to be getting into her lungs. "My father found out you were planning a trip to Mexico and asked you to—"

"It wasn't like that," Cody said flatly. He watched the emotions bruising her eyes and his heart contracted. "Your father came to me. He was worried about you. Apparently, you'd said too little or too much in one of your letters, I'm not sure which. He knew I was on a six-week medical leave from the police force. He offered me a paid vacation in Mazatlán in exchange for a little detective work."

Liza's eyes were wild, almost frantic. "You never told me, not even after..."

The unspoken words hung there in the air between them. Not even after we became lovers. "I wanted to tell you in the beginning," Cody said. "Later . . . it didn't really matter. I loved you, and that love had nothing to do with my reason for being here."

She appeared not to have heard him. She was looking at the bed with dull brown eyes. "He must have paid for everything. This room . . ."

He took her in a gentle grip. "Liza, listen to me. You know me as well as anyone in the world. You've been my lover, my child, my friend . . ." He gathered her close, trying to warm her. "You can't stop believing in what we had."

She held herself stiff in his arms. "Let go of me."

"Why? So you can run away again?"

"What do you want me to do?" She grabbed a hard breath, spoke hoarsely through it. "Do I stay and give you the chance to destroy me?"

"Hell, no!" Cody had never been closer in his life to losing all control. His fingers trembled on her shoulders, his body was rigid. "Whatever you do, don't give me a chance, Liza. I don't expect it from you. You're not willing to give up *anything*—not your freedom, not your independence. No risks, no sacrifices. The rules are hard and fast, and you're not about to let me or anyone else change them."

"I have to protect myself."

"And to hell with everyone else." Despair gave a painful edge to Cody's voice. "Did you think I wanted to own you? You were wrong. I never wanted to hurt you. I only wanted to be *important* to you. I wanted a sacrifice in the name of Cody Davis—some little sign that I was worth more than your precious independence. I should have known better."

She pushed away from him. She didn't want to hurt him, either, but it was too late to prevent it. It was too late for both of them. "I have to go," she whispered.

"Leave, then. I'll give you the only thing you seem to want from me. I'll stand here and watch you walk away. Go on, *leave*."

And she did.

Chapter

9

DENVER, COLORADO, in December—the view from Cody's apartment window was white. White sky, white frosted trees, white sidewalks shoveled out of white lawns. Even the air was white polka dot.

"It's snowing again," Cody said. "A snowplow just came along and buried my Mustang."

"You shouldn't park it on the street." Jenny Shapiro Coulter was on the carpet in the middle of the living room, bending over a tiny pink body on a tiny pink receiving blanket. "I've told you a million times you ought to use the underground parking. That's what it's for." She regressed to a cooing singsong as she smiled down at her bundle of joy. "Tell Cody how silly he is, my little precious, Mommy's little angel pie. Oh, what a good girl. You smiled at me, didn't you?"

"I don't like to park my car where I can't see it. At

least this way I know exactly what's happening to it. It's being buried alive." He turned away from the window, stopping short when he realized exactly what his dear friend was doing. "Ah heck, Jen . . . do you have to do that in here? On my *carpet*? Couldn't you change her diaper in the bathroom or something?"

"On that cold, hard tile floor? Certainly not." She lifted her reflected gaze to his with an ingenuous smile. "I could take Samantha in on your bedspread. It's nice and warm, and then you wouldn't have to witness this embarrassing spectacle."

Cody matched her smile for smile. "Stay away from my bedspread, sweetkins. Friendship only goes so far."

"Mercy on us! Was that a little grin I saw on your face?" Jenny threw back a curtain of flyaway blond hair, squinting up at him thoughtfully. "By George, it was. I'd forgotten what a nice smile you have, Cody. I haven't seen much of it since you got back from Mazatlán."

"You know how it is. The nasty adjustment to reality after a vacation." Cody wandered over to the naked Christmas tree in the corner of the room, pushing his hands into the back pockets of his jeans. "This tree looks sick. It needs something."

"It doesn't take a genius to figure that out." Jenny swaddled baby Samantha in a blanket and popped a pacifier in the rosebud mouth. "It needs decorations, lights, tinsel . . . and an angel. You need an angel at the top."

"I haven't got an angel," Cody said, looking down at the cardboard box of decorations at his feet.

Chaos, total chaos. Strands of Christmas lights were strangling his battered collection of K mart decorations. "This is junk. Why don't we just grab a can of spray snow and slime the thing?"

"Where's your Christmas spirit?" Jenny asked sternly. She got to her feet, jumped over a bulging diaper bag, and jabbed at Cody's chest with one finger. "This Scrooge stuff isn't like you. You *love* Christmas. Remember the mechanical Santa you rented last year and put in front of the building? The one with the hand that went up and down waving at everybody?"

"The snowplow buried him, too." Cody had well and truly lost his Christmas spirit. He had a nagging feeling that he might have left it under the tropical sun in Mazatlán.

Liza. What was she doing right now?

Jenny had known Cody since the days of braces and bubble gum. She had no qualms about interfering in his life at any given moment. That was what friends were for. "So tell me," she said.

"Tell you what?" Cody's tone was abstracted.

Softly. "Tell me what happened in Mexico."

"Nothing happened. I had a great time. It's beautiful in Mazatlán—you and Tony ought to fly down sometime."

Jenny held his eyes. "You're a terrible liar. Why do you even bother?"

"Practice makes perfect," Cody muttered. "Are you going to push this issue, or are you going to be a good friend and let it drop?"

Her expression clearly wondered how he could ask such a thing. "I'm going to push. Silly man. For three weeks, you've walked around with these basset-hound eyes, and it's breaking my heart. I want you to sit down in this nice Berkley recliner"—both hands on his shoulders, she shoved him in the right direction—"and pour out your soul. Think of me as your psychiatrist."

Cody sat in the nice Berkley recliner. Jenny sat cross-legged on the floor at his feet. "This isn't easy," Cody said finally. "Why don't you help me decorate the tree, instead? After all, that's why you came by."

"I came by to probe into your psyche," Jenny said cheerfully. "The tree was just an excuse. Look, maybe I can make this easier. I'll ask the questions, and you just answer yes or no."

Cody slipped lower in his chair, resting his chin on his chest. "What fun," he said tonelessly.

Jenny wasn't deterred. For the first time in her life, she was witnessing the irrepressible Cody Davis in a major navy-blue funk. She wanted to know about the woman who had brought about this astonishing phenomenon. And it *was* a woman; she would bet her life on it.

"We'll start out with an easy one," she said. "Do you love her?"

"Lady, you missed your calling. You definitely should have been a shrink. Such tact, such sensitivity. . ."

"Quit stalling. Do you love her?"

"Oh, hell."

"I'll take that as a yes. Does she love you?" When Cody held her gaze without answering, she said happily, "Another yes. Now we're cooking. Where did you meet her? Oh, never mind, I know that one.

Mazatlán, it has to be. You came back with a terrific tan but a lousy disposition. So what was her name? Amy? Barbara? Christie? Denise? I'll go through the alphabet, and you can stop me when I'm close."

"I hate this game."

"Then tell me what happened in Mexico, and I won't have to harass you like this."

It wasn't easy. Cody began somewhere in the middle of his story, wound around to the front, and briefly touched on the ending. *Their* ending. Jenny listened with rapt attention, chewing on her fingernails and shaking her head.

"Well, you made a hash of it, didn't you?" she said when Cody subsided into silence. "I have to say, though—this Miller person sounds absolutely fascinating. I'd love to meet him."

Cody studied her with a pained expression. "Thank you. I always know where I can go to find a little sympathy."

"Cody, Cody . . . the situation is not hopeless. You fell in love. You went a little overboard, which is quite understandable. You go a little overboard in everything you do, which is why you get shot so often."

"Once. The last time I was stabbed."

"Also there are times when your hormones seem to stage a revolution on your brain."

"Someone has to take charge."

"The thing you have to remember," Jenny said wisely, "is that the opera isn't over until the fat lady sings."

It took Cody a few moments to absorb that one. "Jenny-poo, you've changed one too many diapers."

"I know what I'm talking about. I'm a woman, Cody, I know how women react."

"*Normal* women?" Cody murmured, and was rewarded with a jab on his arm.

"All women. From what you've told me, you and Liza found something very special together. A love like that isn't going to wither up and die just because of a few mistakes. Take my word for it. Tony and I made every mistake in the book, and we still came through."

"You're forgetting something." Cody fixed his gaze on the window, watching the snow mound in drifts on the sill. "Liza is in Mexico, and yours truly is in Denver. You and Tony came through in the same city. You even lived in the same building."

"Details," Jenny sniffed. "It's Christmas, Cody. Be of good cheer."

"Give me one reason why I—"

"*Because* it's the season to deck the halls and trim the tree and roast chestnuts on an open fire. And I'll bet you a turkey dinner with all the trimmings that Liza Carlisle will be home for Christmas."

Cody made a New Year's resolution two weeks early. No more moping. No more worrying. It was Christmas, dammit, and he was going to get into the spirit of the season if it killed him.

He went back to work with a sprig of mistletoe pinned to his jacket. He decorated his locker at the station with a green plastic garland and a strand of blinking lights. He rented a huge plastic reindeer with a light-bulb nose and planted him in the snow in front of his apartment building. He smiled until the muscles in his cheeks seized in a perpetual grin. The days were full. The nights were endless.

A week before Christmas, Cody polished up the old credit card and headed for the department stores. He bought a Barbie doll and a Barbie Corvette for little Samantha. He bought a Lladro sculpture for Tony and Jenny and a ski sweater for his best friend, Jenny's brother, Josh. Everyone else got fruitcakes.

He took his packages home and discovered a plate of ginger cookies swathed in cellophane wrap in front of his door. A Christmas card was tucked beneath the plate: *Season's Greetings to our favorite policeman. Love, The Carlisles.*

The Carlisles. Cody told himself it was only polite to take them a little Christmas remembrance of his own. He stuck a green ribbon on one of his inde-structible fruitcakes and set off for a little holiday visit.

The Carlisle home was the stuff that Christmas cards were made of. The Tudor mansion was nestled strategically in a stand of snow-frosted pines. Two huge evergreen wreaths adorned the double doors. The old-fashioned lamppost in the front yard was striped with red ribbon like a candy cane. Cody had visited once or twice before, but never with butter-flies in his stomach and his heart in his throat. Did he honestly expect Liza to answer the door? She could be in Mexico or Bora Bora or Puerto Rico, but the chances of finding her in her own hometown . . .

Liza opened the door. At least, the startled golden brown eyes were Liza's. Her hair was hidden under a knit stocking cap, and her mouth and chin were bur-ied in several layers of pink-striped muffler. It was a dramatic metamorphosis from the golden-skinned gypsy who had danced the night away in Mazatlán.

"You're here," Cody said slowly, drinking in what little he could see. "Liza? It *is* you in there, isn't it?"

She pulled the muffler to her chin with gloved fingers. "It's me." Two words. All she could manage with the aching knot in her throat. So many emotions were flooding over her, she could hardly separate one from another. Fear. Hope. Despair. Love. She looked him up and down, absorbing the changes that a thousand miles had wrought. Here on his home ground he took on a harder edge that was purely masculine. He wore a sheepskin jacket, well-washed jeans, and heavy cowboy boots. He was wearing his dark hair an inch longer than he had in Mazatlán, and it completely covered his collar in back. He looked so good to her, so fine . . .

"I didn't expect to see you," Cody said. "What are you doing in town?"

Liza's shrug was barely visible in the puffy parka. "It's Christmas. I always try to make it home for Christmas."

"Your parents must be honored." Now why the hell had he said that? The battle light was in her eyes again. Mentally kicking himself, Cody held up the leaden fruitcake. "I came bearing gifts. Your folks left me a plate of cookies. I wanted to say thanks and Merry Christmas."

"They're not home," Liza said.

Cody waited. After a lengthy pause, he replied, "You *could* invite me in. I won't bite."

Liza stepped aside and motioned him in with a visible lack of enthusiasm. She sensed the impending destruction of her fragile composure, slipping through her fingers like so much sand... "How have you been?"

"Can't complain." He caught a whiff of her perfume, which made him smile. He'd been smelling it everywhere lately, whether Liza was present or not. She was haunting him. "What about you?"

"Fine." Liza watched his reflection in the mirrored walls of the entry hall. He looked almost dangerous contrasted against the immaculate white-on-white decor, the elegant furniture, and the pastel silk flowers. For the first time, she could actually imagine him handling a gun, his fingers curved around the cold metal handle, his eyes hard as nails...

"Why are you looking at me like that?" Cody asked curiously.

Liza blinked, feeling herself perspiring inside her thermal cocoon. "Like what?"

"I don't know." He looked irritated, as if the entire tone of the conversation was frustrating him, like a speech that was going sour. "Like you expect me to jump your bones any second. I came bearing fruit-cake, gypsy, not grudges. Peace on earth and all that. I'm on my best behavior this time of year."

"I'm not worried," Liza snapped. "It's very nice to see you again."

"A lovely surprise seeing you, too," Cody ground out. Silence. The grandmother clock in the hall chimed once, twice, three times. "Where would you like this damn—this fruitcake?" he said finally.

"I'll put it in the kitchen. I'll be right back." Liza tromped off down the hall in her rubber snowboots, looking like the Pillsbury doughboy in pink.

Cody took a deep breath, the first he could remember since Liza opened the door. So. The wandering gypsy had come home for Christmas. It didn't necessarily mean anything. Still . . .

He was wired; he couldn't stand still. He wandered into the living room, his boots dragging in the plush white carpet. A tiny splash of green on the fireplace mantel caught his eye. Liza's plant, looking woefully out of place in its little clay pot amid a collection of Hümmel figurines. And it was thriving.

"I couldn't leave it in Mexico," Liza said defensively behind him.

"It looks like it traveled well. Maybe it can be your companion on your travels, a globe-trotting philodendron. How did you get it through customs?" Liza murmured something inaudible. "I didn't hear you."

"Smuggled it!" she repeated, quite loudly. "I wrapped it in a baby blanket and called it Roger."

"Well, what do you know?" Cody marveled, turning his bright green gaze on Liza. "She's made a commitment to a house plant. Will wonders never cease? Do you talk to it?"

Liza answered him with stony silence.

"Well, I wouldn't admit it, either," Cody said cheerfully. He was feeling almost festive. Liza had named his plant Roger and smuggled it through customs. It was a victory of sorts, though he was careful not to look too closely at it. "So. How did the reunion with your parents go?"

"Better than I expected, actually. I promised to be a little more forthcoming about my activities, and they promised not to sic another detective on me. My mother was sincere, my father was . . . apologetic but unrepentant. He keeps asking me how we got along together beneath the tropical moon. I'm afraid your little trip to Mazatlán was his misguided way of playing matchmaker." She met his eyes with a lift of her chin. "I suppose you had to turn in a final report when you came home?"

"They had me to dinner," Cody admitted quietly. "I told them you were healthy and happy and they should learn to communicate without a go-between. End of report."

The silence in the smooth white room became awkward. Liza tried to push her gloved hands in the pockets of her parka, but they wouldn't fit. "I'm hot," she said finally. "I was just going outside to shovel the walks."

"Need some help?" he asked politely.

"I can do it," she replied, less politely. Liza looked at him pointedly, her eyebrows disappearing into the knit cap. His cue to leave.

Cody had never taken directions very well. It was a quirk of his stubborn nature. Tell him to turn left, he'd come up with every reason in the world to turn right. "Then I'll watch," he said.

True to his word, he watched. He leaned against the hood of the Mustang and watched while she huffed and puffed like a steam engine clearing six inches of walk. He watched her snow-clotted cap slip over her eyes and her muffler trail off her shoulder. He watched when she tripped over her own boots and landed on all fours in the snow.

"Need some help?" he asked politely.

"Did I *ask* for help?" She made no pretense at politeness whatsoever.

Eventually, Liza threw off her sodden cap, tossing it into the branches of a pinion pine. The muffler followed. "I'm not a cold-weather person," she muttered. "I miss my bikini."

Cody missed her bikini, too. He was about to say so when he noticed the lemon-sized bruise on her forehead. "What the hell is that?"

Liza's shovel dug into the crusty snow. "Your language is deplorable. What the hell is what?"

"That bruise on your head." Cody stomped through the snow, catching her chin in his hand and tilting it up. "How did it happen?"

She kept shoveling, the first cold breeze of apprehension whispering down her spine. "Miller took me sailing last week. I had a collision with a mizzenmast or a topsail or something. It's nothing."

"Miller's still in Mazatlán?"

Snow flew. "He was when I left."

"Isn't that nice," Cody said with deceptive softness, chucking her gently on the chin. "You are coming along, gypsy. Miller's been down there *three whole weeks*. That must be some kind of a record for you."

He turned and walked back to his car. His fingers were on the handle when the snowball hit him in the back of his head. Hard. He turned slowly, hands clenched into fists at his sides.

Liza had something to say. "You are the most arrogant, mollusk-brained moron I've ever met in my life. Maybe one of these days, when you stop making false assumptions about people, you'll be capable of handling a mature relationship. And that's a *big* maybe, buster."

Cody's head—and his heart—were still smarting. Very deliberately, he scooped up a handful of snow, packing it into a lethal-looking snowball.

"You wouldn't," Liza breathed. "I swear, if you dare—"

The snowball caught her in the shoulder. Even through the layers of downy padding, it hurt.

"If you can't stand the heat," Cody said sweetly, "get out of the kitchen."

Holding his eyes, she dug her shovel into the snow, then lifted it in the air.

"I wouldn't," Cody said . . . and got a mouthful of snow for the warning. In a flash, the Rocky Mountain Karate Classic champion had disarmed Liza of her weapon, and tumbled her into the snow with a neat little foot-sweep. Before she could struggle to her feet, he was on top of her, knees straddling her waist, hands pinning her arms above her head. Her boots kicked the air.

"You," said Cody, "have a nasty temper. Say uncle."

She pressed her snow-wet lips together with a fierce glare. Snowflakes sparkled on her lashes, weighting them.

"Say it," Cody whispered, a ragged edge to his voice. She was twisting her hips beneath him trying to free herself, evoking certain memories that were better forgotten—at least for the time being. "I want you to say . . ." He blanked out for a moment, drifting toward the snowflakes melting on her lips. "Uncle . . . or aunt or something . . ."

Now, only inches separated their burning gazes. Foolishly, Liza recognized a hollow, empty hunger deep within her. The slightest movement from either of them would bring their lips together, and she couldn't afford that, she couldn't fight that . . .

"Uncle," she said breathlessly. "Uncle, aunt, cousin, grandmother—"

His lips closed over hers, touching her with sweetly probing familiarity. His tongue stroked, following the molding of her lips before probing inside with a sudden, fierce need. Her hands were free, and instead of pushing him away, they were tangled in his hair, drawing him closer. She wanted more. She wanted to pull his head to her breasts, wanted to feel his mouth and tongue working their magic . . .

They rolled in the snow, Liza on top, then side by side. Intensive care for a broken dream. The snow might have been the white-hot sands of Mazatlán, deep enough to cover them. Liza swallowed his kisses like cool spring water, each one sating and increasing her thirst. She lost pace with her heartbeat, oblivious to where she was and why she was here.

"I'm staying," she said between heart-stopping kisses. He drew back from her, his hair tumbling in wild and sweet disorder. "What did you say?"

"I'm staying. I'm going to find an apartment after the holidays."

"Liza—"

"I have gainful employment. I used my trust fund to buy a part-interest in a small travel agency. I'm even going to invest in a nameplate for my desk."

She was staying. She was investing in a nameplate. She had named her plant Roger. The clouds began to break, a glimmer of sunlight flickering through. Cody lowered his head in a dreamlike trance, pressing her again and again into his slow, open kiss. She was staying.

He heard the car before she did. "Liza?"

"Hmmm?"

"We have company." He stood, pulling her to her feet, brushing the snow from her jacket and hair. The Carlisles' Lincoln Continental crunched to a halt beside Cody's Mustang on the snow-packed driveway.

Dr. and Mrs. Carlisle had been making their holiday rounds. They were dressed for the occasion, Mrs. Carlisle in a white fur jacket and jaunty fur hat, Dr. Carlisle in a natty tweed jacket and a bright green bow tie.

"Good afternoon," Cody managed huskily, ruffling the snow out of his hair. "I was hoping you'd come home before I left." *Ho-ho-ho* . . . "I wanted to thank you for the cookies you left me."

"You're very welcome." Mrs. Carlisle's startled blue eyes focused on her snow-dusted daughter. "Hello, darling. Pleasant afternoon?"

"We shoveled the walks," Liza said. If either of her fond parents noticed the handle of the snow shovel sticking out of the evergreens or the embarrassing length of cleared sidewalk, they were tactful enough not to mention it.

"Cody, you'll have to come in and sample Charlotte's eggnog," Dr. Carlisle said jovially. "You've never tasted anything like it. Oh, and we have some cold poached salmon flown in fresh from the coast. We're celebrating our daughter's homecoming. Liza's given us the finest Christmas present we could ever have."

Cody's gaze fastened on Liza. "Has she?"

"Yes, indeed. She arrived lock, stock, and steamer trunk last weekend. You can't imagine how pleased we are to have her home again. Those flying visits of hers were never long enough."

"Oh, I think I know just how you feel," Cody said softly, still holding her in his eyes.

"Say you'll come in for supper," Mrs. Carlisle begged prettily. "It isn't often we get to—" She was interrupted by two short blasts from the horn in Cody's car.

"My radio," Cody said. "Excuse me a moment."

Liza was suddenly cold. She wrapped her arms around herself, hugging tightly. Her sweater was wet from the snow Cody had thrown down her collar, and her hair was freezing in blond icicles down her back. When Cody returned, she avoided his eyes, trying to still the chattering of her teeth.

"I have to go," he said. "There's been a problem downtown. Mrs. Carlisle, can I take a raincheck on that eggnog?"

"Certainly. You're welcome anytime, you know that."

He turned to Liza. "We'll talk later."

"You take care of yourself," Dr. Carlisle ordered. "I've seen you two too many times on my operating table already. I don't want to find you there again."

"Believe me, if I have anything to say about it, you won't." Cody's eyes whispered over Liza's features, the velvet of her eyebrows and lashes, the arched cheekbones embroidered with high color, the reflection of the snow in her golden eyes. "I've never wanted to live so badly in my life."

Liza had no appetite for the cold poached salmon flown in fresh from the coast. Her mother began to worry, to question her, but her father interrupted with a gentle wave of his hand.

"Leave her be, Charlotte," he said. "Liza can always raid the refrigerator tonight if she gets hungry."

Liza retired early that night. Her room was a jumble of suitcases and boxes. She cleared a path to her bed, then curled up on the quilted silk comforter and stared at the telephone.

She wanted to call him. She just wanted to hear his voice and know that he was safe. That "little problem downtown" he mentioned could have been anything. She couldn't stop thinking about it. The uncertainty was there all the time, eating at her. There were horrible, vicious people in the world who spent their days and nights doing horrible, vicious things. Anything could happen to Cody, *anything*. It was as if someone had switched the name tags in their relationship with no warning. Suddenly, it was Liza who was brooding and letting her imagination run wild while Cody calmly went about his business. Shock treatment indeed for the wandering gypsy.

The three weeks she had spent alone in Mazatlán had seemed like three years. Cody had left a void in her life that begged to be filled. At times, loving him had been painful, but she began to wonder if it was a pain she could live with. And could it possibly be any worse than the pain of living without him?

Miller had turned out to be a good friend, taking her here and there, trying to get her mind off her troubles with inspired adventures. When he'd nearly killed her sailing to Deer Island in twenty-mile-an-hour winds, he suggested she might want to look into mending her broken heart in a sane and rational manner.

At the moment, Liza didn't feel sane or rational. All she could think of was what might be happening to Cody at this very minute, at this very second. When she made the decision to come home to Denver, she knew she had no guarantees that things would work out between them. But they wouldn't even have a chance to *try* if something happened to Cody. . .

She picked up the telephone book, scanning the listings until she came to Cody Patrick Davis. Her fingers were trembling when she dialed the number.

"Merry Christmas!" Cody's voice, and from the sound of it, he'd just bagged his entire year's quota of bad guys. Obviously, he was fine. Now she could re-vert back to sixth grade and hang up on him. It was tempting.

She sighed. "I'm selling tickets to the policeman's ball."

"Liza?"

"Then again, I might have dialed the wrong number."

"*Liza?* Is that you?"

"Actually, I'm doing a survey on detectives." She took a deep breath. "Calling to make sure everyone got home safely."

He didn't say anything for a long time. When he

did, his voice was edged with gentle wonder. "Well, well . . . I do believe the worm has turned. Liza Carlisle . . . are you *checking up* on me?"

"Of course not. You're a big boy, you can take care of yourself. Good night, Detective."

"Liza?"

"What?"

"How does it feel to let go of some of your caution? Is your heart still beating? Is the world still turning?"

"I'll let you know," she whispered.

Chapter
10

THE FOLLOWING EVENING, Cody and Liza went on a date. A careful date. Liza's teeth began to grind from the pressure the moment Cody picked her up at the door. She wore slacks and a bulky cable-knit sweater that belonged to her mother. She had dressed carefully, bearing in mind her date's possessiveness. Her hair was neatly swept to one side with a french clip —a careful style, not too modest, not too frumpy. Her coat—also her mother's—was nice and bulky and shapeless, guaranteed to hide the body beneath.

Cody underwent his own personality change just for the occasion. In Mazatlán he'd nearly lost Liza forever with his narrow-minded attitudes and irrational jealousy. Tonight was going to be different. Mellow was the watchword. Liza was going to discover that he could be just as charming and laid back as that jerk Miller O'Keefe. And not a word about the future, or commitments. He was going to be very careful about that.

Cody had given a lot of thought as to where he should take her. Finally, he decided on a modern art exhibit at a local gallery, followed by dinner at a brand-new club the boys in the squad room had told him about. He hated modern art, but Liza would enjoy it. Didn't she have a degree in fine art?

Cody set the pace strolling through the art gallery, somewhere between dead still and barely twitching. He wanted Liza to have plenty of time to appreciate each and every exhibit. He didn't want to rush her. He was very careful about not rushing her. Liza had to realize that he was capable of behaving like a perfect gentleman—for one night, at least.

"What do you think of this one?" he asked, stopping before a sculpture entitled *Home on the Range*.

Liza stared with horrified fascination at the papier-mâché figure of a young boy riding a milk can for a horse. His skin was shellacked with a map of the United States, and he wore a ten-gallon cowboy hat studded with rhinestones. The sculpture rested on a platform that looked remarkably like an Amana Radar Range.

"It's like nothing I've ever seen before," she said finally. She didn't want to hurt Cody's feelings. He seemed to be enthralled by the exhibit. "And look here, it's only five thousand dollars."

If Cody hadn't been on his best behavior, he would have rolled his eyes to the ceiling and started to choke. But he was being extremely careful not to do anything crude, thoughtless, or impulsive. "I wonder where you would put it?" he murmured.

Liza had very definite ideas about where it should go, but she refrained from voicing them. "Probably in a family room," she said weakly. "A big family room."

"Probably."

Liza found something nice to say about nearly everything. The effort exhausted her. She was broiling in her mother's sweater, and the tweed pants itched. When Cody announced triumphantly that they had at last seen everything there was to see, she could have cried with joy.

The club Cody took her to had just opened two weeks earlier. It was located in the basement of a warehouse in an area of town that was slowly being renovated. The catchy black-and-white neon sign above the stairwell said simply, FANTASIES.

"I hope I'm dressed for this," Liza said, hearing the music floating up to the street. It was quite loud, actually. Even the asphalt beneath her feet seemed to vibrate.

"You look beautiful," Cody assured her. "You couldn't possibly look anything but beautiful." All evening he had wondered about the slacks and sweater. They weren't . . . Liza. He missed her waist.

The interior of the club hit them like a hurricane. The music was deafening. The air was ninety-five percent cigarette smoke and five percent oxygen. Fifty barrel-sized tables were crammed around an empty stage. Apparently the music was prerecorded.

"The food is supposed to be good," Cody said tonelessly as they found a table next to the stage. "The boys at the station told me you'd love it here."

"I'm sure I will." Liza had just noticed something

rather strange. The majority of the Fantasies patrons were women. As a matter of fact, the place was absolutely overflowing with females of every age and description. "Cody . . . is this a women-only club or something?"

"They let me in," Cody said. "Also three or four other men, but we're definitely in the minority. I'm beginning to have a nasty feeling—"

The tempo of the music suddenly changed. A tall young woman with waist-length black hair took the stage, hips swaying in time to the sultry beat. "Are you tired of waiting, girls? Of course you are! And I won't keep you in suspense a moment longer. Allow me to introduce Andrew the Attorney!"

The crowd went wild. Liza watched with saucer eyes while Andrew made his hip-grinding entrance. He was dressed in a three-piece suit and tie, and carried a thin briefcase. He wore glasses . . . for about thirty seconds. Then, dancing in time to the beat, he slipped off the glasses and gave them to Liza. From that point on, it was all downhill.

Cody was a statue. For some reason, Andrew the Attorney had chosen to play to Liza. He threw her his tie. He dropped his jacket over her shoulders. Liza grew hotter and hotter in her mother's sweater. She studied Cody out of the corner of her eye, inwardly cringing. He'd had that same look when she had danced with Miller. Dangerous.

"I think we ought to go," she muttered, when Andrew was down to his attorney's briefs. "I'm really tired."

"We haven't ordered dinner yet," Cody said flatly. "I'm told their nachos are terrific here."

"I'm not really hungry." Liza dropped Andrew's clothes in a heap on the table. The only thing in her mind was getting Cody out of Fantasies before he lost his temper. This careful date was playing havoc with her nervous system. "Cody? Please?"

Walking to the car, he said not a word. Driving through the snow-packed streets, he said not a word. Liza watched the windshield wipers working tirelessly against the misty snowfall, wondering where it had all gone wrong. The best-laid plans of mice and men...

"Would you like to stop someplace else for dinner?" Cody asked coolly.

"I don't think so. It's getting late."

"Hell, yes, it's nearly ten-thirty."

Thirty silent minutes later, Cody walked Liza to her front door. Her parents were out for the evening, but every light in the house was burning, thanks to an automatic timer. Liza fiddled with the house key for several minutes before Cody took it out of her hand and opened the door.

"Sorry," she muttered. "I'm not used to keys."

"I remember."

Liza bit her lip. "It's been a lovely evening," she said woodenly. "Won't you come in for a drink?"

Cody's smile was plastic. "I don't think so. I'll call you tomorrow." He gave her a breezy, platonic peck on the cheek that reminded her of Miller. "Good night."

Liza closed the door, then nearly jumped out of her skin when Cody threw it open again. He walked past her and into the living room without saying a word. Bemused and more than a little apprehensive, Liza closed the door and followed him.

He was standing in front of the Christmas tree. His leather jacket was thrown over the arm of the sofa.

"So what happened tonight?" he said quietly.

"I don't know." Liza found a little corner of the sofa that felt nice and warm and comforting. She curled into it, hugging her knees against her chest. "I don't know. It wasn't like that in Mazatlán. We weren't . . . uncomfortable with each other. And we smiled. We haven't done much smiling here."

Cody thought of the art exhibit and said grimly, "There hasn't been much to smile about."

The room filled with a dull, demanding quiet. Liza huddled deeper into the couch, wondering what had happened to them. *How can everything change so much in three weeks? We used to have such friendly silences in Mazatlán. But here . . . it's all wrong here.*

"Where do you plug in the lights to the tree?" Cody asked suddenly. "I hate dark Christmas trees."

"The light switch in the corner."

Cody flipped the switch, then methodically put out every lamp in the room. After a moment, the colored lights on the tree began blinking, bathing the quiet darkness in a kaleidoscope of red and blue and green. Cody wasn't feeling particularly festive, but he forced himself to say cheerfully, "A little Nat King Cole on the stereo and we're set. Do you like Nat King Cole?"

"Not much." Liza was tired of being careful. It

didn't help, anyway. "I like instrumental Christmas music."

"Oh." Cody slumped down on the sofa, rubbing the iron knot of muscles at the back of his neck. "It figures."

"What do you mean, it figures?"

"Our tastes are a little different, that's all." Cody looked at her, his eyes reflecting the colored lights. "You seemed to enjoy the art exhibit, and I thought..."

"You thought what?" Liza asked flatly.

"Hell, I thought it was ridiculous. Remember that papier-mâché cowboy riding that milk can? You wanted to buy the flippin' thing for your family room."

Liza sat up very straight, rearranging her spine into a more aggressive posture. "You asked me where someone might put it and I told you. I didn't say that someone was me." She pulled out the french clip in her hair and chucked it halfway across the room. A defiant, absurd gesture, but it felt good. If only she could do the same to her mother's sweater. "I thought the whole exhibit was a little off-the-wall, if you want to know the truth."

The pause simmered with tension. "Why the hell didn't you tell me?" Cody asked with soft deliberation.

Liza shrugged. "You seemed to be enjoying it. I didn't want to spoil your fun."

"What about the strip show?" Cody snapped. "Did you enjoy that?"

"Not really," she said airily. "Andrew wasn't my type."

Taking his time, Cody walked over to the side table, pouring himself a glass of red wine. He downed it in one gulp, catching Liza's eyes across the room. "Don't worry," he said. "I'm not going to drink myself into an embarrassing situation again. I'm just filling an awkward pause in our conversation until someone fires the next shot."

Liza wasn't going to cry. She *wasn't*. "What happened to us?" she whispered.

"I think we're trying too hard." His hard expression softened, a wry smile lifting the edges of his mouth. "True to form. You and I seem to do everything in excess, don't we?"

"I thought if we just gave it another chance..." her voice trailed off miserably. She slashed at tears.

"Liza." Cody was beside her in a watery vision, taking her cold hands. "We're not dead, sweetheart. The situation isn't hopeless. We're just finding our way. Tonight we were afraid we were going to make the old mistakes. Instead, we wound up making a bundle of new ones. It'll be all right."

"Cody, *nothing's* right." She drew back her hands, scrambling off the couch. "I'm trying to be what you want, you're trying to be what I want... none of it makes any sense. I'll never be Donna Reed. I don't *want* to be Donna Reed!"

"Who the hell said anything about Donna Reed?"

"I'm confused," Liza muttered. She dropped her head, buried her chin in her sweater, slammed her hands in the pockets of her slacks—the very picture of dejection. "I'm depressed. I need a bubble bath."

Cody stood slowly, shrugging into his leather

jacket. "Fine. Good idea. Go soak your head. But you're forgetting something, gypsy."

Gypsy. It seemed good to hear that name again. Liza looked up at him through tousled gold bangs. "I am?"

"You am." Two short strides took him to her. His hand slipped through her hair, cupping the nape of her neck, his thumb idly caressing the edge of her jaw. "You're forgetting we love each other. We're going to work our way through these hangups of ours."

"What makes you so sure?" she asked softly.

His smile was vintage Cody, indestructible and oozing with charm. "Charles Bronson always gets the girl. Forget tonight ever happened. Tomorrow we start over, for better or worse. No more pretending. You've already taken the risk, Liza, or you wouldn't be here. The hardest part's over. Now all you have to do is relax and . . ."

Liza closed her eyes, feeling his mouth brush her forehead with a play kiss. "Relax and . . . ?"

"Just let me do my job, ma'am," he drawled. His kiss left her gasping, and there was an ominous quaking in the muscles that supported her knees. She sank slowly down on the sofa, watching the dark-haired devil in the leather jacket stroll out of the room. His hips undulated with easy rhythm, a completely masculine metronome.

That night she substituted a cold shower for the bubble bath.

Two days later, Liza was arrested driving to the City Center mall to buy Christmas presents.

She noticed the flashing red bubble gum machines behind her not ten minutes after she left home. She pulled over to the side of the road, completely baffled. She wasn't going over the speed limit. It was impossible to drive faster than twenty miles an hour on icy roads without skidding out of control. The inspection sticker on her Porsche hadn't expired. What then?

She rolled down her window, smiling at the young policeman in the mirrored sunglasses. "What can I do for you, officer?"

"License and registration, please."

"Was I doing something wrong?"

"License and registration, please."

Liza waited silently while he studied the documents. His jaw was set in stone. Probably a very good poker player, she thought judiciously. He certainly didn't give anything away.

"Do you mind telling me what's going on?" she asked with exaggerated patience.

"I'm afraid you'll have to come with me, ma'am."

Liza blinked. *"What?"*

"You were driving in a reckless manner that would endanger other motorists."

"I was going fifteen miles an hour!"

"You'll have to follow me to the station, ma'am."

"Are you kidding me?" Liza tried her very best smile, dimples galore. "You're kidding me, right?"

"I'm sorry, ma'am. If you'll please follow me . . ."

Liza had never visited the police station before. She followed the police car off the main thoroughfare, through winding residential roads. When the police car pulled to a halt in front of a snow-crusted park, she was baffled. Pine trees and park benches on one side, a two-story colonial on the other. *Hill Street Blues* it wasn't.

The policeman opened her car door and gestured her out. "Ma'am?"

She wished he wouldn't call her "ma'am." It made her feel old. Liza climbed out, shading her eyes against the blinding glare of the winter sun. "Where are we? Is this some kind of a joke?"

"I'm releasing you into his custody."

"Whose custody?"

He pointed, a smile cracking the Clint Eastwood jawline. "His. Good luck, ma'am. You're going to need it."

She saw him then, sitting on a blanket in the middle of the miniature winter wonderland. He was wearing his leather jacket, his dark head gleaming in the harsh sunlight. And even from this distance, she could see that he was smiling.

She walked slowly toward him, the heels of her boots breaking through the crusty layers of snow. He had a picnic basket, and a bottle of wine half-buried in the snow. Nature's ice bucket.

"Merry Thursday," Cody said. "You've just been invited to lunch."

"What do you think you're doing?"

"Me?" He assumed an adorable air of boyish innocence. "Just doing my job, ma'am."

Her smile grew slowly, keeping pace with his. "You're very dedicated."

"You have no idea. Won't you sit down?"

It wasn't a catered lunch. Cody had made everything himself: chicken sandwiches, celery stuffed with cheese, a Thermos full of steaming chili. Hostess cupcakes for dessert, he explained solemnly, because he burned the cookies. Liza had a hunch that he was telling the truth.

She didn't bother to be careful. She talked about Miller, about the hair-raising trip to Deer Island. Cody discovered that he could listen without his temperature shooting sky-high. The fact that Liza had cared enough to come home had taken the cutting edge off his possessiveness. A little encouragement and he was a pussycat.

They watched the children sliding down the hill on giant Frisbees and garbage bags. They lay flat on their backs and found cloud pictures in the sky. They inhaled the crisp, fresh fragrance of pine and newfallen snow. Cody picked up a snowball and Liza told him in no uncertain terms that she didn't feel like a snowball fight today. He smiled and put it down.

It was all over in an hour. Duty called, and Cody packed the hamper with resignation. "I have to testify in court this afternoon," he said. "But before I go, I want to give you your Christmas present. I bought it this morning."

"It's not Christmas yet," Liza protested. "If you give it to me now, I won't have one to open on Christmas."

"Greedy woman." He pulled a small velvet box from his pocket and tossed it to her. "I'm sorry it isn't gift-wrapped. There wasn't time."

She knew what it was. Even before she opened it, she knew what it was. Her hands went clammy inside her gloves, her heart jumped into her throat, and her first impulse was to toss it right back to him.

"Shouldn't we wait until Christmas to exchange gifts?" she asked, her voice edged with desperation. "I haven't got a thing for you yet."

Softly, he insisted, "Open it, gypsy."

She stalled as long as she could. She pulled off her gloves, smoothed her hair, turned the box this way and that.

"I'm going to be late for court," Cody said gently. "The judge frowns on that."

She opened the box with trembling fingers. Oh, her pulse . . . it was a ring. A beautiful diamond set in brushed gold, far too elaborate for a policeman's salary. An engagement ring.

"Cody. . ." She couldn't find the words. She was touched. She was ecstatic. She was *terrified*. "It's the most beautiful ring I've ever seen, but . . . I can't . . . Cody, I'm not ready to wear this. You know that."

"I know that," Cody said calmly. "Look closer."

There was a thin gold chain pooled in the box. Liza picked it up slowly, found that it was threaded through the ring like a pendant. "What's this?"

"Think of it as another necklace," he said helpfully. "You didn't have any problems with the other necklace I gave you, did you? No. That's all this is, another necklace." His eyes went through her like flickering heat. "Until you're ready for something else."

"But what if I can't—"

He stopped her with a hand over her mouth. "Let me do this, gypsy. I've seen firsthand how quickly life can change, how the dreams of a lifetime can be shattered in the blink of an eye. I don't want to have any regrets."

"I don't want to hurt you," she whispered.

His smile was gentle. "It's all part of the game, angel. I've never been afraid of taking risks. I'm not going to start now. Drive home carefully. You don't want to be arrested again."

She stayed at the park long after Cody left. She sat on an icy park bench, watching the children at play. The box was burning a hole in her pocket. *Just another necklace*, she told herself. *That's all it is*.

Who was she kidding?

After an hour, she was joined on her little bench by an elderly man with newspapers stuffed beneath his ragged coat and a bottle of whiskey clutched in his hand. He stared at her with red-rimmed eyes, then tapped her gently on the shoulder.

"Will you marry me?" he asked mournfully.

Liza stared at him. "No, thank you," she said finally. He took it well, lifting the whiskey bottle to the sky with a shrug. Liza stood, brushing the snow off her coat.

Nothing had changed. Cody was still giving her time to explore her feelings, to discover what kind of commitment she was capable of making.

She hoped.

That night the telephone rang at the stroke of midnight.

"I didn't wake you, did I?" Cody said.

"No." There were 629 hand-painted flowers on her bedside lamp. She knew because she had counted them all. "I'm wide awake."

"I thought so. Staring into space with glassy brown eyes?"

"Something like that."

"Where's your new necklace?"

"I'm wearing it," Liza said. The diamond was nestled between her breasts like a baby snowball. "Are all diamonds this cold, or am I having a panic attack?"

"Panic attack," Cody said promptly. "My bed is cold. Do you think I'm having a hormone attack?"

"Now I know what to get you for Christmas. A nice electric blanket."

"Oh, goody. Did I tell you today I love you?"

Liza thought of the surprise picnic in the snow, of the chicken sandwiches with too much mayonnaise, and the Hostess cupcakes. "I think you did," she said softly.

"I'll tell you again." His voice took on a dreamy quality that touched her like a caress. "I love you, gypsy. If I have to give up my work and wear a backpack the rest of my life to keep up with your wanderings, then so be it."

"Don't turn in your badge yet."

"Speaking of which, I'll be out of touch for the next couple of days. We're staking out a small-time fence on the West Side of town. Human, not picket."

"I gathered that." Then, trying to sound casual, she added, "Will it be dangerous?"

"Piece of cake. Meanwhile, you can go out and buy me an angel for my Christmas tree. I have it on the best authority that I need an angel. Try K mart."

"Cody?"

"What?"

"I love you, too."

"I needed that." She could feel his smile through

the wires. "We'll put up my angel together when I get back. Now close your Bambi browns and start the sugarplums dancing in your head. You'll be asleep in no time."

And she was.

Chapter

11

It took Liza two days to find the perfect angel. Eventually, she saw just what she wanted in a handicrafts store in Larimer Square. It was made of porcelain, with hand-painted features and a magnificent silk gown embroidered with pearls. The price was absolutely exorbitant, but the man deserved the best. She could always take a couple of the left-hand digits off the price and tell him she got it at a blue-light sale.

Her mother was up to her elbows in sugar-cookie dough when Liza got home. For the first time in years, Liza allowed herself to relish the pleasure of *home*, the cheerful kitchen rich with the aroma of rising bread and warm cookies, the spice garden in the greenhouse window, the winter world beyond. It was a safe place, a place to stop and breathe and plan. The claustrophobia these walls had once given her was gone, replaced by a gentle comfort.

"You should see the angel I bought for Cody's tree," she said. "It's absolutely gorgeous. It has real pearls sewn on the skirt and made a heck of a dent in my savings account—" She broke off abruptly, staring at the phone. "Did he call?"

Liza's mother smiled, but managed to keep her voice casual. "Who?"

"*Cody*. As if you didn't know."

"I haven't heard from him. Where is this absolutely gorgeous angel? I'd love to see it."

"In the front hall. I'll get it." She grabbed a hunk of cookie dough as she passed the bowl. Less than a minute later she was back, carrying a huge cardboard box with straw spilling out of the seams. "It's a little large. I hope Cody's tree is big enough to . . . Mom? What is it?"

Mrs. Carlisle was just hanging up the telephone. The gaze she turned on Liza was one of surprise and concern. "That was your father. He wants you to come to the hospital."

Abruptly, Liza felt cold. "Why?" she whispered, guessing.

"He didn't tell me much. Apparently, Cody is there. I don't know the details. Darling, would you like me to come with—"

Liza was out of the door before the last word was out of her mother's mouth. She forgot her coat, her purse. She drove the Porsche like a maniac, nearly skidding off the road twice. The diamond ring was cold and hard against her skin. She kept holding it, trying to make it warm.

The girl at the information desk couldn't locate

Cody's name on the terminal. "Sometimes it takes a while to get them into the computer," she said vaguely. "Maybe if you checked back in an hour—"

"Look again," Liza's voice was trembling. "He's a policeman. He came in sometime this afternoon—"

"Liza! I've been waiting for you."

It was her father, his expression revealing nothing. He ushered her away from the information desk, ignoring the almost incoherent stream of questions she threw at him. "Not now, sweetheart," he said evenly. "We really ought to get upstairs. Time is crucial."

They caught the elevator just as it was closing. Two nurses stepped back to make room, exchanging a pleasant greeting with Dr. Carlisle. Liza shifted her weight from one foot to another, watching her father's face with a mute appeal in her eyes. He smiled at her reassuringly, but offered no further information.

The elevator door opened to a portrait of a newborn baby on the wall. Liza barely noticed it. She followed her father down the hallway, passing an incubator wheeled by a young candy striper. *An incubator.* Liza looked at the sleeping baby within the incubator for a stunned moment before she realized where she was. The fourth floor. The maternity ward.

Dr. Carlisle paused before a wood-grained door with white plastic lettering: WAITING ROOM.

"Something's rotten in Denmark," Liza said slowly.

Dr. Carlisle patted her shoulder in his best bedside manner and opened the door. Cody was there, sitting on the orange sofa, thumbing through a dog-eared copy of *Parents* magazine. He was wearing skintight jeans, a black sweatshirt, and a brown leather shoulder holster. He heard the door open and glanced up, a rich smile spreading through two days' growth of beard.

"Finally," he said. "I thought you'd never get here." He dropped the magazine, crossing the room to take her in his arms. Liza made a fist and planted it in his stomach. Cody's eyes stretched as he sucked air. "What was *that* for?"

"Is this part of the game, too?" Liza was rigid with temper. "Did you talk my father into helping you? Did the two of you work this out together?"

"What the hell—"

Liza rounded on her father. "And you! You said that time was crucial!"

"It is," Dr. Carlisle responded calmly. "Even more so as you get older. And now I'm going to leave the two of you to clear up this little misunderstanding."

"You can't leave without explaining," Liza snapped. Speechless, she watched as her father proved her wrong, quietly closing the door behind him.

"*Now* do you want to tell me just what the hell this is all about?" Cody asked flatly.

Liza whirled, her nails cutting into her palms. "Don't you what-the-hell me, buster! You can't do this to people, you can't take their emotions and turn them inside out. Was this little trick supposed to convince me that I can't live without you?"

Cody glanced at the corner chair. A timid-looking fellow stared back at him, *Field and Stream* magazine forgotten in his lap. "Liza," he said calmly, "if you'll just stop and take a few deep breaths, let me take you outside where we can—"

"Well, it worked!" Liza slapped Cody's hand off her wrist. "Your scheme worked. I realized I didn't want to live without you. I also realized *I don't want to live with you!*"

She turned to leave, throwing back her hair in a very effective gesture. In the meantime, Cody's hand snaked out, slipping a cold metal handcuff on her wrist.

"Gotcha," he said.

"What do you think you're doing?"

"It's a matching set," he said grimly, holding up his own wrist. "His and hers. Come on, sweetheart, you have some explaining to do."

"If you think I'm going out there in handcuffs—"

"Save it."

She could have made it difficult for him. She could have dropped to the floor and let him drag her down the hall like a demonstrator from a sit-in. Still, something told her that she would only slow him down. By the look on his face, nothing short of a firing squad could stop him.

Cody hauled her into the first empty room they passed. He closed the door with his foot, then sat down hard on the bed. Under the circumstances, Liza had no alternative but to sit down hard on the bed beside him.

"Talk," he said.

"Is this how you arrest people? If this is how you arrest people, I'm surprised you haven't been sued for—"

"*Talk.*"

He looked sincerely confused. He sounded sincerely angry. Liza had the uncomfortable suspicion she might have been jumping to conclusions. She felt rather like someone who had plunged into the deep end of a pool and then remembered being unable to swim. She looked down at her steel bracelet and said falteringly, "My father called home. He said you were hurt...well, he said you were here, and I should come down. Then when I saw you sitting there in the maternity waiting room, I thought..."

"You thought?"

"I thought it was a trick."

"A trick," Cody repeated tonelessly. "Something to make you realize just how much I mean to you? Something to make you understand how precious life is when you have someone you truly love?"

"Something like that," Liza said miserably. "Although now I can see that my father—"

"Your father," Cody said, "is ruthless. Liza, two hours ago I happened to witness a minor traffic accident near the pawnshop we were staking out. The driver of one of the cars happened to be a very pregnant woman, and the shock of the accident sent her into labor. Yours truly delivered a bouncing baby boy in the back seat of an unmarked police car. When I brought the new family to the hospital, your father kindly offered to call you and ask you to meet me here. I had no idea he would look on the situation as a heaven-sent opportunity to play Cupid. And I certainly didn't deserve the fist you buried in my stomach."

"No, you didn't," Liza said miserably. "I don't know what came over me. I'm sorry."

"You're forgiven. You're cute when you're hysterical. Now do you mind if I ask you something?"

She bowed her head over the handcuffs, rubbing a smear from the silver metal. "What?"

"Bearing in mind that I'm completely innocent of your father's scheme, tell me something... Did it really work?"

Liza slowly lifted her watery eyes, her thoughts scattering like dead leaves in the wind. Cody returned her look, every ounce of love he felt shimmering in his forest-green gaze. His smile was crooked.

"Yes," she whispered.

"You love me."

"Oh, yes."

His smile touched her heart. "What a battle you fought, gypsy."

She wiped her tears away with her free hand. Where were they all coming from? "If we ever have children," she said defiantly, "I swear to you I'm going to tell them everything. How you had me arrested, how you took me to see Andrew the Attorney, how you handcuffed me and dragged me around the hospital..."

"You don't want to do that," Cody said soothingly. His lips touched the curve of her cheek, then brushed the soft corner of her mouth. Amusement danced with the fierce desire in his gaze. "Besides, by the time we have children, I'll have given you so many wonderful memories, you won't even remember the nasty old handcuffs. How many do you want?"

Liza lifted her chained wrist. "One set per family

is plenty. Could you take these off, please?"

"Not handcuffs, gypsy. Children. How many do you want?"

"Are you trying to push me again?"

Cody flashed the smile that she loved, the one that made it hard for her to breathe. "Who, me?"

Second Chance at Love

COMING NEXT MONTH

RELEASED INTO DAWN #440
by Kelly Adams

Annie Maguire has been waiting for
Esteban Ramirez to come back for more
than a year. Old friends, he returns to her
with a startling confession. He's loved
her all these years. Now Annie must
make a confession of her own…

STAR LIGHT, STAR BRIGHT #441
by Frances West

Single mother Marjo Opaski is
drawn to handsome Matt Rutgers. But
her daughter is more than a little wary. Why
does her mother suddenly have stars in
her eyes? And can Marjo really let
herself risk being hurt again…

SECOND CHANCE AT LOVE

SECOND CHANCE AT LOVE
